# A VERY DEAD CHRISTMAS
## A ZOMBIE ANTHOLOGY

EDITED BY
ANTHONY GIANGRGORIO

Copyright © 2014 Undead Press
ISBN Softcover ISBN 13: 978-1-61199-096-6
ISBN 10: 1-611990-96-3

For more info on obtaining additional copies of this book, go to:
www.undeadpress.com
Cover art by Jason Mooers

# Table of Contents

More Zombie/Christmas anthologies
you will like!


"Christmas is Dead" from Living Dead Press.com
"Christmas is Dead. . . Again!" from Living Dead Press.com
"An Undead Christmas" from Undead Press.com
"Dead Christmas" from Open Casket Press.com

Available wherever books are sold!

# THE FIGHT BEFORE CHRISTMAS

MICHELE ROGER

'Twas the night before Christmas, when all through the house,
The children were running. I was ready to pounce.
The shotguns were loaded by the chimney with care,
In hopes a final stand was survivable there.

The kids hid in closets and under their beds,
While visions of corpses danced in their heads.
Mama with hatchet and I with heat packed,
Had just settled in, waiting for the attack.

When out on the lawn, we saw they were gathered,
I shot out the window, raining glass as it shattered.
Away was the window, through it I dashed,
Killing a zombie, we collided and crashed.

The moon on the chest of the dead zombie foe,
Glistened with intestines as they oozed in the snow.
When what would my terrified eyes should behold,
The zombies had double and tripled ten fold.

My smart little boy was so clever and quick,
He gathered what ammo and guns he could nick.
A shot gun, an Uzi, a semi-automatic,
Ten gauges, a magnum and a Kevlar jacket.

From the top of the porch, the undead would walk,
"Shoot your gun! Hurry up! Now, shoot them all!"
As rotting brains that before the bullet deluge fly,
Sent their bones and their teeth and their heads to the sky.

Then up to the roof top, my son and I flew,
Holding our own against a zombie or two.
 Out of nowhere, they began to surround us,
Climbing the gutters, now more were behind us.

As I gathered my son and was turning around,
Down the chimney we fell while firing off rounds.
At the hearth stood a zombie decaying head to foot,
Enormous, advancing, he rendered me mute.

A bundle of toys, mama threw at his back,
But he ravaged our dog like he was opening a pack.
His eyes how they twinkled, his dimples, how merry,
Blood soaked with sinew, his nose a rotten cherry.

His droll gaping mouth, our dogs fur with a bow,
Mixed into his beard as he dealt his death blow.
The collar of the dog he held in his teeth,
His meal bought me time to regroup and think.
Taking my shotgun, I aimed at his head,
Firing wildly, filling him with lead.
He was chubby and plump, a right jolly old elf,
I laughed as he died, in spite of myself.

As my son kicked his eyes, my wife chopped his head,
Soon gave me hope that Santa was dead.
I spoke not a word, but went on to work,

Creeping through the house, killing zombies that lurked.

Emptying my rifle, my killing continued,
While my wife and my children hoped to be rescued.
By midnight, exhausted I was the hero,
It was dad with fifty and zombies, zero.

By shooting, beheading and undaunted fight,
There would be Christmas by morning light.

# I'LL BE HOME FOR CHRISTMAS

KELLY M. HUDSON

They went back every year at this time, giving themselves almost a week for travel. The only reason they knew this was the right month, the right day, was because of Julie. She kept the calendars—and she was accurate.

Clinton led the family. He had since Father died, and Father had made him promise to keep just this one tradition alive, if he did nothing else. He told Clinton to bring the family home, every Christmas. Bring them home so they could remember how things used to be, before the dead rose, before the world fell apart, before mankind turned against one another.

Clinton kept his promises.

This meant packing the family into the SUV and gathering enough supplies to last for the trip there and back. This meant guns and ammo, but it also meant water and food. The folks at Alpine Gap didn't appreciate them taking the food, although the water wasn't a problem. But Father had been a Founding Member of the Gap and so it was understood by everyone that this was a condition of his family staying there. His family was valuable.

Oldest daughter Julie was the Timekeeper. Martha the youngest taught the kids mathematics during their school hours. Darren, the one in the middle, just now turned sixteen, was really good with guns, maintaining and keeping them in great condition. And Clinton, well, without Clinton, the lights wouldn't stay on and the vehicles wouldn't stay moving. Clinton meant everything to the Gap and was a big reason why the Council didn't want him to go.

"I promised my father," he would tell them, and they would listen. They would grumble, too. But they would let him go. They always did. Every year, though, it got worse and worse, harder and harder. Soon, he figured they wouldn't let him leave at all, even though he'd taught others the basics in case anything ever happened. People were like that, however; they stuck with who and what worked, and whether this was superstition or not, it was the reality of the situation. They simply didn't want him to leave.

Clinton was twenty-three now and hadn't known much of a world outside of the apocalypse. He was fifteen when it all went down and he had to grow up quickly. He learned on the fly, as did his Father and Mother, how to kill the walking dead and how to procure needed supplies and how to sustain the family. Father and Mother led, and they leaned on Clinton to mind the children, to keep them safe and get them ready. This wasn't easy to do, but he managed. Somehow, he managed.

They went on the run, leaving their house behind, Father vowing to return someday.

"We'll make it back, regardless of the dead or the living," he'd said. He'd worked too hard to buy this house, this piece of land to call their own. He wouldn't give it up so willingly.

Life on the road was hard. Everyone knows the stories of the survivors. Not only were there the living dead to deal with, in all their masses, but the cannibals, and the homicidals, and the rapists. So many threats. So few people to trust.

One day, they found the perfect location. Alpine Gap. There was already a community there. It was three hundred miles from their home, up in the mountains, where it was always cold, and the freezing temperatures kept the dead at bay. For some reason, the cold made them slower, less hungry, less ambitious. So they didn't find many zombies where they now chose to live, only the occasional straggler.

Humans came, though. They were relentless for a time. But soon that tapered off. They formed the Council, and Father got the machinery tied to the dam working again, and once they had electricity, their situation changed forever. Within a year, they became a functioning community, with the ability to raise some cattle for their needs and to farm some crops in the greenhouses they built. All of this was because of Father and Mother's ingenuity.

The first time they went home for Christmas was the most terrifying. They had been at Alpine Gap for eight months and were getting used to the relative safety there. But Father was insistent, even if Mother and the Council disapproved. Father took only Clinton with him the first time. They would prepare the way, Father said, and prepare it they did.

They stole back into their home town, traveling back roads in the jeep they'd initially escaped in. They had weapons and food and water—and Father had a plan.

It was easy to get there. Most of the main roads were clogged with dead cars and dead corpses. They avoided them. They took country roads where the living had always been sparse, anyway. It was the same route they'd used to flee. They snuck into the suburb on foot, carrying the basic supplies with them, and Father used the house key to let them in.

There were zombies, of course there were. But they were slow, and by then Father and Clinton were good with knives. They stuck the ones they needed to and avoided the rest. Getting to the front door had been no problem.

The house was as they'd left it, and when Clinton stepped inside, he felt an awful pang in his heart. It was as if he were walking back into a dream he'd had the night before, a pleasant and wonderful dream. It was the happiest place on earth. But this dream was a lie. It told of things how they used to be, not how they were now.

It almost hurt too much. Clinton wanted to flee, but Father's hand fell on his arm and guided him up the stairs to his old bedroom.

The sight of his bed, his toys, his posters, his old computer, made Clinton weep. He sat and cried and Father held him. When the tears subsided, Father told him his plan.

The next morning, they went to work.

In the basement were the decorations. They carried them to the living room and set up the plastic tree, the same one they'd used all his life, and strung the lights and hung the tinsel. Father plugged the lights into the battery pack he'd brought and they sprung to life; reds, greens, blues, yellows, all dancing and bright, cheery, as if it really was Christmas out there, and the world was as it had always been.

Before they went much further, Father stapled black garbage bags over the windows, hiding the lights so they wouldn't attract attention. The zombies came anyway. They were at the boarded-up windows and the reinforced door.

What drove them, what gave them the ability to perceive when a human was nearby, no one ever understood. What was irrefutable was that the dead were always there, ready to feed. Even as time went by and they rotted more and more, they still came, unrelenting, always hungry.

Father and Clinton sang a couple of hymns that first night, ending with 'Silent Night'. But the night itself was anything except silent. The living dead were at the boards over the windows and door, scratching, moaning, ever-present.

They turned out the lights and crept quietly upstairs; they slept in their own rooms. At first Clinton didn't want to be left alone, but after a few moments, he was glad for it. For just a few hours, he could pretend things were as they used to be. But even though it hurt to do so, he was happy for the first time in a long time.

By morning, the zombies had mostly dispersed, although there were a few stragglers. There were always stragglers. They took down the lights and tinsel and packed everything back into their respective boxes except for the tree.

"We'll leave it like this," Father said. "So when we return next year, your Mother, brother and sisters can do the decorating."

They slipped out the back, making sure everything was locked tight and secure. On their way to the Gap, they stopped and took their time, clearing the country roads of any abandoned vehicles to make their return path easy next year.

When next year arrived, they came back home and it was a joyous occasion. There were even less zombies this time. Mother and the children were so happy. They stayed a few days until Christmas was over and then packed up everything.

"One day," Father said. "We'll all come back here to live, forever. This is our home, and no zombies will ever stop us from living here."

This repeated the next year and the next and it got so that Christmas was something they all looked forward to again. Each of the family made little presents for the others and hid them in sacks they carried when they went back home, and each year, the number of zombies was fewer and fewer, and they could sing louder and longer without paying much attention to the dead.

They were safe. This was their home, and Christmas was their favorite holiday.

Sometime during the next year, Father had a heart attack and died. They put a bullet through his brain to keep him from coming back. Clinton had the local doctor embalm the body as best he could, to preserve Father, so that they could take him home the coming Christmas. That holiday was a solemn affair. They buried Father in the backyard next to the shed he'd built with his own two hands only ten years before. There was much weeping.

Mother died shortly thereafter. She lost her will to live. Some say it was heartbreak. Clinton didn't know. He just understood that they would have to repeat the process again the next Christmas and he wasn't happy about it.

Months later, he dug back into Father's grave. He put Mother next to him and covered it up. Before they went home, he carved a stone with their names in it, as well as their birth and death dates. He placed it above their heads on the ground.

That Christmas was hard.

The next was tough, but better. It was just the kids now and Clinton was in charge. They did things exactly how they'd done them before, only this time it was Clinton promising they would one day come back here to live, forever, because it was their home.

So now here it was, two years later, and they were going home, most of them grown or well on their way. It would be their final trip.

* * *

"This will be the last time," Clinton said.

Martha, who had her nose stuck in a book, looked up, eyes wide.

Nathan said nothing. He stared out the window, watching the countryside.

Julie stared at Clinton. "But it's Christmas," she said.

"Yeah. This was what Dad wanted," Martha added.

"Mom and Dad are gone," Clinton said. "We need to think of ourselves."

"You said we'd always come back, that we'd move home again," Martha said.

"We will," Clinton replied. "But later, when it's completely safe. Right now we have a new home, at the Gap. People care for us there."

Nathan crossed his arms over his chest. "I don't want to talk about this," he said and kept looking out the window.

Clinton decided to let it go. They were still too young to understand. He had been just like them, up until when he had to bury Mom. After that, things changed. Sure, he wanted to go home for Christmas, but it wasn't home without Mom and Dad. Not anymore.

There was no resistance on their drive. The roads were deserted. The toughest part was finding the road at all. Grass had taken back its natural space and there were patches where he lost the highway completely. This was yet another reason to stop coming out here. Soon, there would be no road at all.

Once he almost rammed into a ditch. They would have been in deep trouble if that had happened, too. But he avoided it, cursing beneath his breath and thanking God at the same time. On another long stretch, a herd of cattle had taken to grazing where the road ran through, so he had to go slow, winding between them, stopping several times to wait until they moved out of his way. He feared running into another ditch by going around, and there was no way he was going to lay on the horn. Even though he didn't see any zombies, he didn't want to take the chance on attracting them.

He pointed all of this out to his brother and sisters but they met his logic with blank stares. They were still too young, he said to himself again. They would come to understand.

What normally took a couple of days now took four, and the longer they were out on the road the more danger they were in. He kept driving as long as he could, pulling over and taking cat naps now and again. But he was too nervous to stop for very long. Nathan offered to drive, of course, but Clinton was having none of it. "You'll be old enough soon," he said.

Eventually, they made it home.

The street was as it had always been, although with more grass and weeds and even a couple of trees sprouting up in the middle of Elm Street.

Some of the houses had been broken into. He could see new windows that had been shattered and doors that were once closed were now knocked off their hinges.

Scavengers.

He kept a sharp eye out but saw no more sign of them. Part of him hoped they had hit their house, too, and stolen everything from the place. This would be another good reason to stop coming. Even Nathan would have to agree with that logic.

But their house had been untouched, as always. It sat a little ways separate from the others in the neighborhood, on a small hill, and had always been shrouded by trees. Now that nature was taking back over, the grass had grown so tall that he couldn't see the old mailbox by the driveway anymore. Hell, he couldn't see the driveway.

Clinton drove around back. There was no way of knowing a house was hidden back there unless the person tried to find it. He circled through the neighbor's yard—he and Father had taken out the fences long ago—and parked behind the garage. Their back-yard was grown over, all except by the shed, where the tombstone was. Clinton made sure to clear that immediate area every year so the family could pay their respects.

Everyone piled out of the van but they were careful. They'd been through this routine many times before. Each of them carried a gun and knife, and there would be no thought of unpacking the van until knowing the house was secure.

Clinton stood by the open driver's door, looking at his old neighbor's house. A tree had fallen over at some point and crushed the southwestern part of the home. Had it been a storm? Did the tree just get too old and give way? He had no idea. It was a miracle it hadn't happened to their home yet. He added this to his list of reasons to make this the last trip.

His siblings waited by the back door for him. He was always the first to enter. Taking the key from his pocket, he inserted it. The lock clicked. So it was still locked; a good sign. He opened the door. It creaked. He'd have to oil it again. It seemed every year he was oiling this door.

The inside of the house smelled like it always did on first arrival—like dust. And old. The air was stale and the interior was dark. He turned on his flashlight and shined it around. The kitchen was the same as he'd left it, except for a small nest in the far corner. It was filled with mice, and the moment the light hit them, the rodents scattered quickly. He cursed under his breath as he shined the light around until they all disappeared into cabinets or down the hall.

He stepped into the kitchen and left the door open, letting fresh air blow inside. Standing in the middle of the kitchen, he listened. He heard nothing, not even the squeaking of the retreating mice. After waiting a few moments, Clinton continued to the hallway.

This was the hardest part. The walls were lined with pictures of the family, from back in the old days. He hated to see the images of his father and mother, so much younger, so happy and full of hope and excitement. What a cruel world to take such things from them and replace it all with monsters and horror.

Well, they were beyond caring now.

Several rooms branched from the hall. The first was the bathroom, on the right. A quick check saw that it was empty. The next was the bedroom Julie and Nathan shared. It was just as they'd left it. The next was Martha's room and again, it was fine. The last was the living room. He crept inside, shining the light around.

Something felt different though, and he wasn't sure why. Everything seemed to be as it had been when they departed last year.

But there was something…off about it. He stood in the center of the room, shining the light around, trying to determine what it was that bothered him. Clinton listened, but there was nothing.

Finally, when the light splashed on the Christmas tree, he realized what it was: it had fallen over. It was leaning against the old TV set. He crouched down and checked its base, determining that a screw had come loose and caused it to tilt. This would be easy to fix.

On the other side of the room was the stairs leading up to the bedrooms and bathroom upstairs. He took it slow and sure, keeping his gun in one hand and the light in the other. It was pitch dark inside because of the plastic garbage bags he and Dad had put up years before; it kept the light out and in.

There was nothing amiss upstairs. The house was the same as it always had been. He went back down to tell the others. This was going to be their last Christmas here for some time to come, maybe forever, and he wanted to get on with it.

He walked through the backdoor with a grin on his face. That grin froze. Three men and one woman were holding guns on his brother and sisters.

Something moved next to him and he heard a loud crack. He saw a bright light and everything went black.

*  *  *

Clinton woke to the sound of laughter. Had he fallen asleep? Were they starting the celebration without him? He heard a deep voice and immediately thought of Father and became really excited. Dad was there with them!

He opened his eyes and the room spun. It was full of bright, cheery lights; the Christmas tree lights. Music also filled the air. The small radio/tape player they brought batteries for every year was playing Christmas songs, via a cassette tape. Things were like they always had been, only when he looked around, he saw that the people in his house weren't family at all. They were strangers.

One of them was holding a knife to Nathan's throat.

"Try that again, you little snot," the man said. He was short and round, not necessarily fat, but thick. He had a full head of bushy black hair and a thick mustache. "And I'll cut you open and drink your blood."

"Lanny will do it, too," one of the other men said. This man was tall and skinny and his head was shaved clean. He had bright blue eyes that shone like diamonds. "I've seen him. Lanny'll drink anything. Sometimes I think he's a vampire."

"Quiet, Tom," a deeper voice said. This was the voice that sounded like Clinton's father.

Clinton turned to look at who was talking. The man sat on the edge of the couch, a bottle of whiskey in his hand. He was sullen and had mean eyes. There was a scowl etched on his face that looked permanent, like his skin hadn't known any other shape since birth. He was glaring at Clinton, appraising him. "Looks like our little lord has finally woken up," the man said. "My name's Reese. I'm the guy who owns this house now."

"What's going on?" Clinton asked. His head was pounding.

"I'll tell you what's going on," Reese said.

A scream rang out from upstairs. Clinton looked around. He saw all his family with him in the living room, all except Julie…

"That's George up there," Reese said. "He's raping your sister. It's been a long time since George had any tail, so he's making himself happy. You can't blame the man, can you?"

Tom snickered. "I got dibs on next."

"You ain't got dibs on nothing," Lanny said. He took the knife from Nathan's throat and shoved the boy into the middle of the room. He landed in a jumble next to Martha, who was sitting still, holding her palms against the sides of her ears.

Julie kept screaming. It was the most awful sound in the world.

Reese laughed. "So you're some sort of hero, huh?" he said to Clinton. "I can see it in your eyes. You're thinking of a way to get free and get back at us. Not gonna happen, son."

Reese looked over to Clinton's left and Clinton followed his gaze. A woman was standing there. She was tall and thin, her face sunken like someone had taken a hammer to the middle of it. At one time, Clinton thought, she might have been pretty. Now she was just ugly. She was holding a gun and it was pointed right at Clinton's groin.

"Cindy here, she don't like men much. She puts up with us because we respect her. But give her a chance and she'll shoot your pecker off," Reese said with a grin.

Julie was screaming and screaming.

"Make them stop!" Nathan shrieked. He turned to Clinton, to his older brother, to do something about it. But Clinton could do nothing. He was as trapped and helpless as the others.

Nathan screeched loud and long, and Lanny bounced from his chair and hit Nathan on the top of his head with his gun. Clinton heard something crack in his brother's skull and Nathan sagged to the floor, like his bones had suddenly gone soft. He lay down on his side, his eyes rolled up into the back of his head, and blood trickled from his nose.

Martha threw her body across Nathan and hugged him, shielding her brother from another blow.

Lanny grumbled and sat back down. "Stupid kids," he said.

Clinton tried to sit up but everything spun again. He nearly fell to the floor next to his brother. Cindy laughed. She sat at the end of the couch where Clinton was laying, keeping the gun pointed at him.

They listened for a long time as Julie's screams filled the house. Eventually, mercifully, they died off.

A few minutes later, George made his appearance. He was a fat man with a red face and a beaming smile. He was missing half his teeth. He had a short shock of red hair on top of his head, and he laughed and slapped five with Tom.

"How was it?" Tom asked.

"She was so tight," George said.

They laughed again.

Clinton wasn't sure if he was going to scream or burst into tears.

"She's upstairs if you want a go?" George said.

Tom shook his head. "Lanny's got next."

"I ain't goin' yet," Lanny said. "I want her to cool off some. Let the blood dry a little, that way I can break it all open again. There was blood, wasn't there?"

George grinned from ear to ear. "Lots."

Tom pointed at little Martha. "Maybe we should have a go at her next."

"You idiot!" Cindy snapped. "She's just a girl."

Tom shrugged. "So was the other one."

Martha jumped up suddenly and bolted out of the room. All of the intruders gaped with surprise before Reese barked out orders. "Go get her, idiots."

Tom and George ran from the room while Lanny stood up, hitching his pants. "Maybe I'll go on up," he said.

"You do that," Cindy added.

Clinton saw his chance. Despite his dizziness, despite the pain in his head, he scrambled to his feet and launched himself at the woman. He caught her in the side, lowering his shoulder and cracking her ribs. She grunted and fell, the gun falling from her hands. Clinton reached for it but she managed to kick it away. It slid across the room. He came up in a fighter's stance, but Cindy was ready for him. She kicked his shin and then his knee. The room spun again as he staggered backwards, in deep pain. He was bunching his shoulders to charge her once more when Reese kicked him in the groin from behind.

All the fight left Clinton. He crumpled next to Nathan, his testicles throbbing as if they'd been dipped in acid.

Outside, a gunshot echoed through the empty neighborhood.

Upstairs, Julie started screaming again.

Clinton began to cry.

Reese sat back in his chair. He produced a toothpick and went to work on his teeth. "Life's a bitch, son." He laughed and shook his head. "You and your family, you look like you've had it pretty good. You're soft. I bet you found a good place to live with a bunch of nice folks. Well, I'll tell you somethin', kid, the rest of the world's not like that at all. It's survive as you can. More often than not, your best friend is gonna become your enemy, come the day the food runs out. But me and my crew, we learned how to work it. We learned how to make it." He leaned forward and flicked the spittle-flecked toothpick at Clinton's face. It struck Clinton's cheek and fell to the floor. "Too bad you ran across us."

Julie kept screaming.

Moments later, Tom and George returned. They dragged Martha's dead body between them. Blood was dripping from her chest and her shirt, which had been yellow, but was now stained a deep crimson.

"I guess we won't be takin' turns on her," Tom said.

"Dump her in the kitchen," Reese ordered. "We'll chop her up in a few." He looked back down at Clinton. "We found a grill in your shed. Does it still work? Got some propane left in it?"

Clinton said nothing.

Reese shrugged. "Go on out in a minute, Tom, and look at it. Maybe get it running. We could have ourselves some little girl steaks tonight."

Tom grinned.

"I call dibs on the butt cheeks," Cindy said.

"You're nasty," George said.

Julie's screams stopped.

An eerie silence filled the house. They all listened, freezing where they were. Everyone sensed something was wrong, something was off.

A loud thump crashed on the ceiling above them.

"Lanny?" Tom called out. There was no response.

Reese looked at George and snapped his fingers. George was running to the stairs when Julie appeared, as if from nowhere. She was naked and streaked with blood and claw marks. Black bruises splotched her chest and legs, and long red welts striped her skin. Her long hair hung over her face and was dripping with sweat. In her right hand she held a bloody spring, the end pointing up.

"Oh," George said.

Julie leapt at him before George had a chance to pull his gun. She buried the pointed end of the spring into his neck and tore it to the right, gashing open his artery. Blood jetted from the wound and George fell backwards over the couch, grasping at his neck. Julie rode him down, stabbing at his face repeatedly. She tore chunks from his cheeks and ripped his nose open. His lips were shredded in seconds and all the while he held his throat, eyes wide with shock.

Cindy was the only person to respond. She pulled her gun and shot Julie in the stomach. Julie looked up at her, surprised, and snarled. She tried to leap at the woman but her feet slipped in George's blood and she fell to the side, sliding off George's plump belly and onto the floor. She felt around at her stomach and started laughing.

Cindy stepped forward and put a bullet between Julie's eyes. Her brains splattered across the floor, painting the bottom of the Christmas tree with red and grayish chunks.

Reese stared at the carnage. His eyes went from Cindy to Tom and back again to George on the floor. "Go check on Lanny," he snapped.

Cindy ran up the stairs. There was a long moment of silence.

Clinton lay on his side, gasping for breath, crying for Julie. Both his sisters were dead now. Next to him, Nathan stirred. At least he still had his brother.

Nathan rose to his knees. He looked down at Clinton, a thin line of dried blood splitting his face in half like a bolt of lightning. Clinton had seen eyes like that before. They were blank eyes, dead eyes. Nathan was a zombie.

Nathan stood up. Tom didn't pay any attention; he was still busy staring up the steps, wondering what kind of news Cindy was going to bring. Reese saw Nathan stand but thought nothing of it. He was just a concussed little boy, for all he knew. Not one of the living dead.

Clinton scooted away, towards the couch. He looked around for a way to escape.

Nathan flung his body onto Reese, who was still sitting at the edge of the couch, whiskey bottle in hand. Despite his tough talk and vicious facade, he was taken by surprise when Nathan's gnashing teeth bit him in the neck.

Reese screamed as the blood gushed from his wound. He slapped at the undead boy burying his teeth into his neck and tried to push him away, but Nathan had reached up and clawed a long strip of flesh from Reese's weathered face. The man stood and staggered, trying to shake the boy loose, but Nathan hung on, gnawing deeper and deeper into the crook of Reese's neck and scrabbling at his face with his free hands.

Tom turned around and drew his gun but there wasn't much he could do. If he shot at all he would hit Reese, and he couldn't do that. Reese was their leader. So he hesitated.

Cindy appeared on the steps behind Tom. She put her hand on his shoulder and Tom jumped. He spun around, frightened, and fired his gun.

His bullet tore a large hole through Cindy's stomach, spraying the stairs with her intestines and a thick wad of blood. She staggered in place, dropping her gun, and picked at the ruins of her guts. Her fingers were slicked with her greasy blood. She held them up to take a good look, as if to convince herself that it was all really happening. Then she sat down on the steps, squishing a large chunk of her intestines beneath her butt. She leaned against the wall and closed her eyes.

While this was happening, while Tom was staring dumbfounded at what he'd done to Cindy, while Nathan was busy feasting on the jittering Reese, Clinton scrambled for Cindy's gun. He grabbed it, letting the weapon fill both of his hands, and came up firing.

His first shot missed Tom. The second one did, too. But the third round clipped the man's ear and Tom shrieked, raising his own gun. Clinton's fourth shot somehow struck Tom right between the knuckles of his gun hand and the man dropped the gun. Clinton's fifth shot sparked dust from the ceiling, missing everything.

Tom turned and ran. He made it as far as the kitchen before it became his screams that filled the house. Clinton just watched, staring into the darkness of the kitchen, gun pointed at the doorway. He never heard the back door slam or any indication of Tom's escape. He did hear the scream, however, and the sound of Tom striking the floor. What followed was a clatter of stomping feet and then a sickening silence. Clinton didn't move. He waited until Martha staggered from the kitchen, her face washed in blood, little giblets of flesh hanging on her chin and pieces of hair stuck to her cheeks. Her hands were soaked with blood. She walked over to where Nathan was peeling back Reese's scalp in an effort to get to the man's brains. Nathan's tiny hands clawed at the skull, tearing long strings of flesh free. 'What Child Is This' began to play on the radio. Its soothing tones filled the house.

Clinton, all hope lost, turned the gun on Cindy and blew her brains out as she began to rise, her eyes now as blank as Nathan's had been. He stepped over his feasting brother and sister and went into the kitchen, shooting Tom in the head before the man could revive. Then he walked back into the living room and put a bullet into George's head. He climbed the stairs and found Lanny lying on the floor. His stomach had been ripped open by the spring Julie had evidently torn free from the bed and used on him. He sat up, his eyes blank. Clinton splattered the man's filthy brains on the wall. He descended the stairs, numb. There was nothing left inside of him, nothing to live for. He stared at Martha and Nathan as they dug out the brains they'd managed to scoop free after smashing in Reese's skull, thereby assuring he wasn't going to be coming back from the dead.

Clinton closed the back door, locking them all in. He stumbled back into the living room, tired, so very tired, and lifted Julie's corpse up and placed it onto the couch in a sitting position. Then he sat down next to her. *I'll Be Home For Christmas* started on the radio. The blinking lights of the Christmas tree twinkled on all the carnage and gore, glinting and dancing across the blood.

Clinton put the gun to his head.

They would all stay here forever for Christmas, he decided.

He pulled the trigger.

# THE ZOMBIE WHO ATE CHRISTMAS

TONY GARCIA

Every living person in the town loved Christmas a lot.

But the Zombie, in the cemetery above and to the north of town, did NOT!

The Zombie hated Christmas! The whole ridiculous season.

There was no need to ask why. He was a zombie after all, and that alone, defied reason.

It could be he hated it all since he was forced to hide in the night.

It could be, perhaps, his hunger for brains just made him long for a bite.

But, I think, the most likely reason of all,

May have been that his dead heart had shriveled two sizes...two sizes too small.

Whatever the reason, his dead heart or his hunger,

He stood there on Christmas Eve, waiting to tear them asunder,

Staring down from his grave, hate slavering from his blackened lips,

At the warm bodies below, dreaming of their blood soon to bathe his fingertips.

For he sensed everyone down in the town below, like a moth to a flame,

Was busy now, with decorations, and preparations, ignorant of the coming pain.

"Tomorrow they hang their stockings," he thought he said, but merely growled,

"Tomorrow's Christmas!" he meant to yell, but instead only howled.

Then, his decaying fingers twitching, he turned back to his empty grave,

"I MUST devour their flesh I so crave!"

For tomorrow, he knew, all the tasty girls and boys,

Would wake to the morning's sun and rush for their toys!

And then! Oh the noise! The sounds! The blood! The brains!

Brains! Brains! Brains!

That's one thing he craved! The BRAINS!

BRAINS! BRAINS! BRAINS!

Then the living, young and old, would sit down to their feast.

And they'd feast! Oh, how they would feast! Oh, how he wanted to feast!

FEAST! FEAST! FEAST!

They would feast on cakes, pies, puddings, candies, and succulent beast.

The hunger was something the Zombie couldn't stand in the least!

But above all of that, then the living would do something he liked least of all!

Every living soul in the town, the old, the young, the tall, and the small,

Would stand close together, with those damned bells ringing!

Hand-in-hand, one and all, if the bells weren't enough, they would start singing!

Horrible noises! Bells and singing! He needed to hear their screams!

SCREAM! SCREAM! SCREAM!

The more the Zombie thought of this disgustingly cheerful Christmas thing,

The more the Zombie thought, "I must devour the whole damned thing!"

"Why, for how many years have I put up with it now?"

"I MUST destroy this...this Christmas...but how?"

Then he had an idea—a gruesome idea.

The Zombie had a HORRIBLE, DREADFUL, DELIGHTFULLY EVIL IDEA!

"I know now what I must do!" the Zombie choked in his throat.

So he dug up the grave of a long buried store Santa—just to steal his hat and coat!

Dry and horrid noises erupted from his lips. He tried to laugh, but the sound was just sick.

"With this outfit, I will become the walking dead Saint Nick! All I need is a reindeer..."

The Zombie looked all around. But, since reindeer aren't buried here, there were none to be found.

Did that stop the rotting Zombie? No! The Zombie simply said,

"If I can't find a reindeer, I'll make one from the dead!"

So he dug up some bones, looted the corpses, then found some red thread,

He tied them together, complete with finger-bone antlers on top of its head!

Then he gathered rotting bags and musty old sacks,

On a ramshackle sleigh made from caskets and corpses he piled the stacks.

Then the Zombie yelled, a noise sounding like "GRAUAP", and the sleigh started down,

Towards the homes where the living lay asleep in the quiet little town.

All their windows were dark, each unknowing that death rode on the air.

All the living dreamed sweet dreams about nothing without care.

Then the Zombie came to the closest house, on the outskirts of the town square.

"This is the first stop", the crusty old Zombie sputtered and hissed,

He scrambled like a spider to the roof, rotten sacks in his fist, and slid down the chimney. For a half-rotted corpse, this was quite a cinch.

If a fat-ass Santa could do it, he thought, then so could a Zombie, in a pinch.

He lost a decomposing body part, maybe two.

Then he stuck his head back on as he crawled from the fireplace flue.

As he twisted on his skull, he saw above him were stockings, all hung in a row.

"These socks," he snarled, "are useless to me, empty of either foot, or toe!"

Then he stalked and crept, with a rotting smile beyond unpleasant,

Around the whole room, stealing each and every present!

Toy guns! Action figures! Drums that bash and horns that toot!

Video games! Popcorn! Even the brick-hard inedible cakes made of fruit!

He stuffed this all in his bags. Then, for a Zombie, moving rather nimbly,

He crammed all of his ill-gotten gains up and out of the chimney!

Like a snake he slithered towards the bedrooms. There he would start a real feast!

He ate the mother like pudding! He ate the father like a rabid beast!

He cleaned out their brain buckets in a maddened state.

Why, then the Zombie devoured the children in his haste!

His hunger far from stuffed, he sprang to the chimney with glee.

"And NOW!" grinned the Zombie, "I will decorate that damned tree!"

With that the Zombie gave father's innards a yank and a shove,

And then heard a small sound, like a dying gasp of a flightless dove.

He turned to the noise, and saw the younger sister of the two!

Standing there was little 'who-gives-a-crap what her name was,' that's who!

The Zombie was caught by this tiniest of things, the youngest daughter,

She'd crawled into a nightmare, when all she wanted was water.

She stared at the Zombie, now covered in blood, and said, "Santa...but, why?"

"Why are you hanging those nasty gross things all over our tree? Why?"

That old Zombie was not very smart, being covered in gore and ick,

He thought of a lie, but ignored it just as quick!

"Why, my sweet..." the words mumbled through blood not yet dried,

And with a grunt and a growl, he ripped her to shreds and decorated the other side.

Affixed to the branches, bits here and bits there, "What a dear,"

As he mounted her head to the top of the tree, "You look lovely, right here!"

No fib to fool a child, just a rotting smile, so glad she was dead.

Then he took another drink, from the corpses still in their bed.

When the last of the house was in shreds, with a cackle he looked up,

Then drained the last contents of mother, from her own coffee cup!

Down the chimney blood dripped atop the log in the fire,

He watched as it popped, and it hissed, then thought, "At least I'm not a liar!"

On the walls he did smear gore and entrails, then stood back to admire,

The mess he had left, the destruction and chaos, and this was just the first house!

With a lurch and a stomp he even managed to crush the life from a small, tiny, mouse!

Then he did the same thing to all of the others, nestled in their houses,

Slashing, munching, pets to children, husbands and their spouses!

Soon it was nearing the dawn... All the corpses, lying still in their bed,

All the living, torn apart by his lust, left in place as he packed his sled,

He packed it with all their presents! The glitter! The roast beast with all the trappings!

The tags! The tinsel! The shiny boxes and their glittering wrappings!

Back up the hill, to the cemetery far up high, no hint of guilt, not a single concern,

At the top of the summit, the peak near his grave, he would watch their Christmas burn!

He hummed and he laughed, fresh blood through his corpse drumming,

The Zombie ate Christmas and no more joy was coming!

"Now they should be waking up!" he thought, considering what they would do.

Their dead mouths slack open, minus a jaw or two.

He thought of their cries, their pleas, and laughed out a, "Boo-Hoo!"

"There's a noise," grinned the Zombie, "That I finally WANTED to hear!"

Silence all around, then a murmur stirred and a faint sound reached his ear.

Over the fire he started and the howls of the wind, a sound carried through the snow.

It started so faint, so low. Then, it began to grow.

But the sound wasn't sad, it wasn't singing, it was groaning, a sound quite merry!

It couldn't be so, not in all his decaying years, not since he was dead and buried!

He stared down below, the amazement so much that he popped from his head one of his eyes!

It made him shake, this new discovery, this incredible surprise!

Every person in the town, the tall, the fat, the short, and the small,

Was shambling! Twitching! Crawling! Moving with no pulse at all!

He hadn't stopped Christmas from coming! For once, and just for him, IT CAME!

A freak of nature, a fluke in the system, but it came just the same!

And the Zombie, jaw dropped slack, standing up to his knees in the snow,

Stood puzzled, confused, "Is this real?" How can this be so?"

"I ate most of their families! I ripped them to pieces! I tore them to rags! Christmas was destroyed! I have all their packages, boxes, and bags!"

He puzzled for hours, until his rotted brain was too sore.

Then the Zombie had an idea, something he'd never dreamed of before!

"Maybe Christmas," he thought, "isn't trapped in a song or bought in a store.

Maybe Christmas...perhaps, now...means a hell of a lot more!"

So what happened next?

Well, in a town full of zombies, no one can say,

But the Zombie who ate Christmas, became Santa Claus of the dead that day!

Suddenly his brain didn't hurt, his skull no longer felt so tight,

He raced down the hill, a load of gifts in tow, cackling madly at the new morning light.

He gave back their gifts, then pulled from his sack, the few living neighbors to share a great feast!

And then the Zombie himself, with a smile so very wide, carved the fat and squirming Mayor, just like a roast beast!

# THE ZOMBIE CHRISTMAS HOEDOWN

## A Walking Fred and Joaquin Dayd Adventure

### JOHN SKERCHOCK

The Reconstruction was going on. The greatest effort to retool the United States since the American Civil War was in full swing, and volunteers were working nonstop around the clock to bring the country back to life. The plague was under control, but there was still a lot of work to be done. It didn't stop during the holidays; for many people the holidays had no meaning anymore.

Fred Burns was one of those people.

It was no secret that Fred hated the holidays, especially Christmas. He never said why, just that he'd rather be working. No one ever asked him because Fred wasn't the kind of man to be questioned. He'd led a hard life and it was visible in the lines on his face and the calluses on his hands.

The heavy winter snows had yet to settle in West Texas, but the winds were strong enough to chill the average person to the bone. Fred pulled his parka a little tighter as he sat in the back of the convoy truck. He watched the flatlands go by behind him, mile after mile, as the man next to him snored away. Soon, Fred would once again walk the interstate because of so many vehicles lying abandoned on the interstate. Now it was all so much scrap metal, just sitting there until it was hauled away by the reclamation teams. But now the highway was patched and serviceable, making Fred's job easier and aiding in the country's recovery.

The big truck began to slow. Fred could see by the green signs that they had come to his exit. He zipped up his parka and pulled a wool hat over his head before tying the hood. He put on his gloves and was ready for the stop.

As the truck came to a stop, Fred got up and crawled out of the back. He grabbed his backpack and slung it across his shoulders, then grabbed the other bag, a big canvas one bulging with assorted contents. When he had all of his gear, he walked to the shoulder and signaled to the driver, who was watching him from the side mirror, to go ahead. As the truck pulled away, Fred turned and began walking down the off ramp to the broken highway below.

He took his time, not seeing anyone waiting for him. His assigned partner had yet to arrive. Typical, thought Fred, it was probably some young kid with no respect for the rules. So there was no need for him to rush. He'd just have to stand around at the bottom of the ramp waiting. But as he got there, he looked down the road and saw a red car parked next to a recharging station, and a tall man standing beside it. The man waved and Fred walked over to him.

The man was a few inches taller than Fred. He was a lot thinner, too, and younger by twenty or so years. He was dressed in black, wearing a Stetson and long leather coat to protect him from the wind.

"Adios, amigo," the man said with a smile.

"Howdy," Fred said, shaking the proffered hand.

"I see we are to be partners on this great mission."

"Yep," Fred said.

"You are Fred Burns, no? You are legend. You have crossed most of this country on foot what, two, three times?"

"Never. Just parts of Arizona, Texas, and New Mexico."

The tall man began to laugh. "Well, a legend must start somewhere. Anyway, I am honored to be working with you. My name is Joaquin Dayd."

Fred scratched the stubble on his chin and asked, "Walking dead?"

"What?"

"You said your name was Walking Dead."

"No. No. Joaquin—WAH-KEEN-Dayd."

"Walking Dead; that's what I said."

Joaquin rolled his eyes. "Madre Dios."

"Look, ain't my fault ye can't speak the language."

Joaquin opened the trunk of the car and Fred tossed his gear in. "Shotgun," he said.

"What do you mean? Of course you ride shotgun. I have the keys."

"I know. I know. I'm usually riding in the back of the truck so I thought it'd be funny to call shotgun."

"Si. Si. It is hilarious. Now come on while we still have light."

"Relax, Sibbly ain't that far away. I been through there once or twice."

Joaquin unhooked the car from the roadside charger and put the cable away. He took off his coat and threw it in the back seat, then got in and sat behind the steering wheel.

"This one of them fancy new cars?"

"No. It is three years old but runs very well for an electric car."

"Well, at least it's American made."

"Everything is these days," Joaquin said. Both men were aware that China was still dark. Between the dead things and the warlords fighting with each other, the country had reverted back to a feudal system, unable to handle the demands of a new society.

They headed south on the empty highway, carefully avoiding huge pot holes and crumbling bridges. The road wasn't a high priority on the government maintenance list. Only interstates and city roads received regular maintenance. Outlying areas still had a way to go before they would get any serious attention.

"You been to Sibbly before?" Joaquin asked.

"Yeah, seems to me it was a small town and they took care of their own. They didn't like outsiders bein' around even if they were only deliverin' the mail, so I made my stop then just moseyed along."

As Joaquin drove, he tried to engage Fred in small talk but the burly man rarely spoke except to offer a grunt or two. After an hour, they came to an exit and Joaquin asked if they should turn or continue.

"Go right," Fred said. "Then right again and we should soon be there."

The road quickly deteriorated into a crushed stone drive before becoming dirt. No satellite antennas could be seen anywhere and no charging stations were available should their car need one.

"Lucky I checked the battery before we left. We might be here a while."

"Wow," Fred said. "Bring her to a stop."

"What do you see?"

"Did you just say 'What Jew you see'?"

"Yes? What do you see?"

"I ain't a Jew, damn it!"

"Who said anything about Jews? I asked what you were looking at."

"You need to learn English so you can speak it!"

"Hey, I speak fine English. I was born and raised in this country. I speak English very well."

"Sure you do." Fred opened the car door and got out. He was looking at a field off to the left; there were two human shapes in it bent over, as if digging into the earth.

Joaquin exited the vehicle and stood beside Fred. "Madre Dios."

The men began walking slowly towards the shapes. Fred opened the right side of his parka and placed his hand on his gun. Joaquin already had his drawn and was covering the shapes.

The two men crept up on the dead things from behind and watched as the creatures tore into the flesh, from the stomach and chest, of a man dressed in a clown costume. A red helium balloon was tied to the clown's left hand, floating a foot above the chaos.

"Odd, I didn't know them things ate clowns," Fred said.

"Why wouldn't they?"

"Don't clowns taste funny?"

Joaquin rolled his eyes and shook his head. "Amigo, you take the one on the right and I will take the left."

Both men fired their needle guns. The sharp hiss of compressed air caught the creatures' attention, but before they could react their heads exploded and they collapsed on the clown beneath them. Fred fired a needle into the clown's head and watched it explode.

Joaquin returned to the car and removed a small box from the trunk. When he rejoined Fred, he opened it and spread the white powdery contents over the three bodies. Fred stood back and Joaquin lit the powder with a cigarette lighter. The sudden *whoosh* almost knocked the two men over, as the bodies were instantly consumed in a big ball of flame.

"Well, that will let them know we're coming."

Fred only nodded in reply.

A few minutes later, the men were driving up to the gate that opened the way into Sibbly. A guard came forward. He looked like an ordinary cowhand dressed in blue jeans and insulated denim jacket and hat. He carried a .22 caliber rifle and wore a Bowie knife at his side. "You two responsible for that fire back there?"

"Yep. Two dead folk munching on a clown."

"Damn! That was Charlie Watkins. He got drunk last night and wandered off. No one discovered him missing until about an hour ago."

"Well, he is ashes now. May we enter?"

"Sorry, we're closed for the Christmas hoedown," he said. "Come back tomorrow."

"Can't," Fred yelled from the passenger seat. "Got mail fer ya. I need to pick up yours and head on out."

The guard bent over and looked through the driver's side window. "Fred? That you? Haven't seen you in forever. Sure. Sure come on in. You can tell us the latest news while you visit." He opened the gate and the vehicle drove through.

"I notice there are no satellite antennas anywhere. Nothing off the water tower or the church steeple."

"Just like I said in my report. Isolationists," Fred said.

America was filled with communities trying to remain apart from the United States. Their leaders claimed it was the government that had brought the plague down upon them. They believed that by disassociating with the mainstream, they would survive and prosper. It was the job of Joaquin and Fred to bring those towns back to working together so that the country could rebuild. It was hard work and Joaquin wondered if Fred was still up to the task. Fred looked beat and angry. He knew Fred had no time for him, but the burly man was one of the few willing to work over the holiday, and the job had to get done.

They pulled up to the post office. It was now a fortified building like several other stone buildings in town, its original purpose lost in the struggle for survival. They were greeted by several townsfolk dressed in their Sunday best with weapons at the ready. "Merry Christmas," they said.

Fred caught the irony and chuckled. Joaquin laughed with him and wished the people a good holiday in return.

"We have mail for the town." Fred pulled the white canvas bag out of the trunk.

A tall, balding man in white slacks and jacket came to greet them. "Howdy! I'm Mayor LeForge of the Louisiana LeForges."

"How do you do. I am Joaquin Dayd and this is my partner, Fred Burns, of the Los Angeles Burns." He wore a wide grin. He had no idea where Fred was from but he felt a little show of his own was in order.

"Well, Joaquin, it's a pleasure to meet you," the mayor said. "We all know Fred. He's been here before. But you're new to us. Is the mail delivery picking up?"

"Ah, yes, Mayor. Our nation is growing strong again and we need people like you and your community to pitch in and help make it great."

The mayor stood for a moment and then grinned. "A salesman! I love it. Come on in. We're about to have Christmas dinner. You can give us your pitch then." He turned away and walked back to the old post office.

Fred followed, and whispered to Joaquin, "We ain't wanted here."

Dinner was served that night in the town hall. All of the residents were said to be there. Joaquin counted eighty three people and noted the lack of minorities, no doubt a result of the race wars that took place in the south after the plague.

The meal consisted of ham and stewed vegetables, with an assortment of dried fruits and fruit pies for dessert. Hogs were abundant in Texas, since there were so few people to help control the population. In some places, they were more dangerous than the walking dead. The ham smelled delicious but both Fred and Joaquin abstained from eating any. Both men had seen their fair share of burning flesh to lose their taste for eating meat. They had some vegetables and hot tea, satisfied with that.

Mayor LeForge introduced the travelers to the town folk. He told them that the two men would offer a presentation before the dancing began. Fred sat in his chair, arms across his chest, looking half asleep while Joaquin stood and talked. He told the townspeople of how America was rebuilding. He spoke of the various safety measures taken and how people were free to roam the streets in many parts of the country. How the cities were once again safe and that the government was moving to do the same for the smaller communities. Already Dallas and Waco were vibrant communities with plenty of jobs and assured safety.

Many people seemed excited. A lot asked questions, but no one seemed willing to make a commitment to get back to civilization. They liked being off the grid. Their power was locally made by windmills, and they had no television or internet services so they didn't have to worry about any place in the world except Sibbly.

Mayor LeForge thanked the travelers for their speech and the mail. Both men declined an invitation to stay for the dance. They were tired, so an aide escorted them to a small house at the edge of town where they could spend the night. In the morning, they would be free to leave with mail for other parts of the country.

"They are hiding something," Joaquin stated.

"Yep. And it's gonna stay hidden, too, unless they want us to find it."

"I don't like this."

"Hit the sack. Maybe we'll learn more in the morning."

* * *

Joaquin woke with a start sometime after midnight.

"Merry Christmas, Walken," Fred said. He was standing in the dark and looking out of the window.

"It's Joaquin! And why are you looking out that window?" He sat up in bed. "It ain't Jew. It's pronounced 'you.' Can't you get my name right?"

Fred said nothing in reply.

"What you are doing over there?"

"I'm watchin' a parade."

"What?" Joaquin climbed out of bed and stood beside Fred. His jaw dropped as he watched the townspeople outside. They were all dressed in white robes and carrying lit candles. They were marching from the town hall to what looked like a one-room school house. No one had a weapon, at least none visible.

"Something is up, no?"

"Yes," Fred replied.

Both men put on their clothes and checked their pistols. The Disney Mark VI needle gun was the safest, surest weapon on the planet for destroying zombies. The pistol used compressed air to shoot up to one hundred explosive needles at a speed of one hundred and forty-two feet per second, to pierce the skull of a human being with a measured accuracy of thirty feet. Once inside the skull, a small charge in the needle exploded and destroyed the brain. The only concern was making sure there was enough compressed air in the pistol so that it could do its job. Both guns were in working order.

"Let's go," Fred said.

The men left their room and the house they were in without being detected. They made their way to the school by staying mostly in the shadows. Once there, they checked the area for a way to get in. The windows were covered but there was no guard outside. Something was happening because there was a lot of noise coming from inside. After a quick discussion, they decided on the obvious approach.

Joaquin crept to the front door. It opened easily. Both he and Fred entered and saw that the townspeople had formed a congregation facing the front of the large room. The mayor was leading the people in a number of Christmas carols. The air smelled heavily of scented candles and something else. It was the sticky sweet stench of rotting flesh!

Joaquin started to grin and was tempted to join in when he noticed the scowl on Fred's face. "What is wrong with you?" he whispered. "It is Christmas."

Fred just scowled. "There are dead things here."

Joaquin shook his head and turned back to face the mayor. That's when he saw it. To the mayor's left was a jail cell door blocking the hallway, and behind it were the animated dead. They were leaning forward, pushing against that heavy metal door, trying to reach the tender living flesh on the other side. Yet Mayor LeForge and the people kept singing as if the dead weren't there.

A little girl in the front row ran forward and tossed a piece of ham between the bars. A long arm reached out and tried to grab her; she giggled and ran away.

"Madre Dios!" Joaquin exclaimed loudly.

People closest to him heard his exclamation and turned around. The singing soon stopped as all the people turned to face the travelers.

"How dare you interrupt our Christmas services!" Mayor LeForge shouted.

"Sir, do you not know the law concerning the living dead? They are to be exterminated upon sight, not kept in cages for your amusement!" Joaquin was livid.

"These are our kinfolk; our brothers, sisters, mothers and fathers. They're not evil. Evil has been forced upon them. They're to be forgiven. This is Christmas!"

"Aye, a time of rebirth and renewal, not the celebration of death," Fred said.

"You're outsiders here. You don't understand. Grab them!" The mayor directed several large men to the task, but before they could act, a loud crash came from behind the mayor. The cage door had fallen off of its makeshift hinges and the dead were pouring out of their confinement.

"Run!" someone shouted and mass panic enveloped the school. Only Joaquin and Fred kept their wits about them. Quickly, they moved forward, fighting through a panicking crowd.

Before they could get to the front, Joaquin and Fred saw that several of the undead had already grabbed two senior citizens and were tearing them apart. Another zombie had cornered a woman and was reaching for her throat as she screamed in terror. Joaquin aimed his pistol and shot the creature in the head. The woman moved quickly out of the way, but only ended up in the hands of another zombie; she was torn apart in seconds.

"Now we got us a hoedown!" Fred yelled.

One by one, Fred and Joaquin fired into the undead horde, destroying one dead thing after another. Fred counted twenty zombies before he was interrupted with a blood-curdling scream from behind him. It was the mayor. He was felled by two dead children who had crawled under a row of desks to bring him down. As their tiny hands plunged into his chest and stomach, Fred destroyed the mayor and his small attackers with shots to the back of their heads.

Joaquin covered Fred from attack, and he dispatched one creature as it was ready to pounce on a distracted Fred.

"It's shit like this that makes me want to take out the whole damn town," Fred said.

"What?" Joaquin didn't quite believe his ears.

"Ya can't fix stupid, so we might be better off not havin' any stupid people around at all."

"Si! But it is Christmas!"

"Yeah, it is," Fred said as he destroyed the last of the living dead while Joaquin fired a needle into LeForge's brain.

When they were done and the survivors were all accounted for, Fred torched the school house with all of the corpses still inside.

The next day, before they left, Fred retrieved the mail while Joaquin consulted with the leader of the survivors. They agreed to reunite with their country. Joaquin fetched a computer and battery pack from the trunk of his car. He set it up and taught some of the people how to use it. He told them that in a few weeks the military would send trucks with supplies and additional radio and computer equipment to help them.

That afternoon, as the two men sat at a charging station off the interstate, Joaquin pulled out a bottle of tequila from under the seat of the car. "Merry Christmas, amigo!"

"Bullshit."

"Why do you not like Christmas so much?"

"Someday when I know you well enough, I'll tell you." Fred took a big gulp of tequila and swallowed it down.

Walking Fred and Joaquin Dayd; saving the West one zombie at a time.

# HOME FOR THE HOLIDAYS

MARIAH DEITRICK

The thought of spending even one minute with Varla Grimes made me wish I were going to have my eyes drilled out. Mother-in-law from hell didn't even cover that woman. She was in a class of her own, and somehow I'd been suckered into spending three days alone with her.

"She's lonely, Maddy," Mark had said after I expressed my many concerns about him not flying out with me. "We're all the family she has left since Dad passed. Give her a chance. She wants to build a relationship with you, and I want her in our lives. But if this doesn't work out, I'll never ask you to go again. I'll cut her out of our lives for good because I won't let her run you off like she has everyone else important to me."

I'd given that woman more chances than she deserved, but in the end, guilt was what landed me in a cab outside the Victorian home my husband grew up in without him by my side.

"It's only three days," I told myself. Mark would rescue me in seventy-two hours. I could survive until then.

With a sigh, I slipped the cab driver a couple of bills and slid out of the backseat with the small suitcase I'd brought with me. Before I made it to the sidewalk, the cab driver sped off down the darkened street, leaving me with no other option than to go inside. Though there had been many chances to back out, and I'd seriously considered each one of them, now it was too late.

The porch light came on as I moved up the walkway. I knew from past visits that this was an automatic response to movement, not a welcome sign from Varla. In fact, I was surprised she hadn't turned it off so I had to stumble around in the dark, while she watched from one of the windows. That was the sort of thing a woman like her did, not have a light that automatically turned on for visitors.

When I reached the door, I paused. Did I knock or just walk in as if I belonged? I almost laughed at myself for even considering that I belonged at this house, so I knocked.

Varla flung open the door, her hair tousled, her dress askew with a sleeve torn at the seam, and a rip up the thigh of her skirt. "You're early, Maddy," she snapped while frantically smoothing her tattered dress. "You should have called."

I glanced down at my watch. I had arrived a half-hour early. I hardly considered thirty minutes a need for a phone call, unless…I glanced around her. "Do you have a man in here?" I couldn't picture Varla with another man, hell; I barely understood how Frank had put up with her for almost forty years.

"Don't be ridiculous. I don't hop in bed with every man I meet. That's how women catch that AIDS stuff and become all skinny and sick looking." She glanced up and down my one hundred and ten pound frame with accusing eyes.

I sighed and fought back the urge to lick my finger and rub it on her face. With what little she obviously knew about AIDS, she would probably rush right to the ER and demand an HIV test. Although that would be hilarious to watch, I knew Mark wouldn't appreciate me sending his mother to the hospital within minutes of arriving at her house.

"Can I come in or do you need a minute to clean yourself up?" I asked in an attempt to change the subject and behave myself.

"Of course. I didn't invite you all the way here so you could stand on the porch." She stepped to the side and gestured me in. "You can take yourself up to Mark's old room while I put myself back together. Meet me in the kitchen and I'll make you a good, home-cooked meal. I'm sure you haven't had one since the last time you visited."

Varla closed the door and headed up the stairs to her room without another word.

Nice welcoming, I thought, but I wasn't expecting anything less from Varla Grimes. Actually, I hadn't anticipated the torn clothes, but the attitude was spot on. Why I came to put up with this, I had no idea. Mark said she wanted to make amends, but I didn't see that yet. As far as I knew, she wanted to get me alone with her so Varla could get all her nasty comments out before her son came for Christmas.

With a sigh, I headed up to the room that never changed. Walking into the bedroom was like taking a step back in time. After eight years, Varla hadn't changed one single thing about the room. Everything Mark had left behind still sat in the same place it had been left, including a pile of laundry in the corner. Though I suspected, since the room smelled wonderful, that Varla had washed the clothes and tossed them back in the same place.

The room had always secretly given me the creeps because it reminded me of a show I'd watched once about parents with abducted children. Most of them kept their child's room the same for when they finally came home.

One mother had left her daughter's room intact for thirteen years before the police found her remains and confirmed she wasn't coming home again. But Mark wasn't missing, so I didn't understand why Varla hadn't turned his room into a craft room, home gym, or at the very least, a spare bedroom with new décor.

Not wanting to disturb the shrine to my husband, I put my suitcase down on the floor next to the bed and took my phone out to call Mark. I didn't call from the airport because I didn't want him to hear the unease I felt about meeting his mother in my voice. But I knew that if he didn't hear from me soon, he might call in

SWAT to check on us. I had to keep the conversation short, however, or he might catch on that I still didn't feel comfortable or want to be there.

"How's it going?" Mark answered on the first ring, clearly anxiously awaiting my call.

"I just got here. Your mom's freshening up while I settle in, but she offered to make me something to eat." I tried to focus on the positives instead of concerning him with all the horrible details of the awkward greeting.

"Good. I'm happy you two are getting along." He sounded relieved. "But if you need anything, you call me. I can be on the next flight if necessary."

"Don't worry. We'll be fine," I said because I didn't want him to sit up all night concerned with what was going on here. I'd have loved to tell him to hop on that flight and meet up with me, but that wouldn't help anything. I had to do this on my own. "So I better get going. You're mom went to a lot of work to cook for me. I don't want to be rude and keep her waiting. I love you and I'll see you in a couple of days."

"I love you, too. Have a good night and call me first thing in the morning."

"I will." After hanging up, I sat for a long moment. I wasn't about to unpack. I needed all my stuff in one place in case I couldn't deal with Varla's shit and had to make a quick escape. Not that it would be the first time I'd stormed out in a hurry after we'd been in an argument. Poor Mark wanted this to work since he was caught in the middle, so I would do my best to keep my cool.

With a groan, I stood, shoved my phone in my back pocket, and went to face my horrible mother-in-law in the kitchen. I had a good idea what to expect, but I wasn't about to hide in the room until Mark arrived. I agreed to this, and I would do my part to make it work.

Varla was bustling around the kitchen when I entered, stirring a steaming pot on the stove, adding more ingredients to it, and shoving something into the oven. The kitchen smelled amazing. My stomach snarled in response.

"Did you get all settled in?" Varla asked without taking her eyes off the bubbling pot.

"Yes," I lied.

"Great!" She continued to shove more in the bubbling pot. "I hope you like beef stew."

I nodded. The new navy dress must have come with a new attitude. Since I sensed no hostility from her, I asked, "Would you like some help?"

"No!" Varla snapped. Her angry expression made me take a couple of steps back. "I don't want you messing things up. Besides, this is a family recipe and you're not family."

So much for the new attitude, I thought, but I let her rudeness slide and silently went to sit at the table. After taking a seat, I watched in silence as Varla shoved a pan in the oven and stuck a lid on the pot. She grabbed the apple-shaped timer, which blended right in with the rest of the kitchen décor, and set it.

"Dinner will be ready about nine-thirty," Varla said. "A little late, but I had to rearrange my day around your flight."

"I'm sorry you felt the need to change your day around my arrival." I wasn't about to apologize for my flight time, but like the pot on the stove, I started to bubble over with anger. I had to let a little steam out or I might explode.

"Like I had a choice," Varla snapped. "It's a good thing I can adjust to whatever's tossed at me. That's part of being a great mother and wife, which is something you haven't figured out. At least my son has me to care for him the way you can't. And I thank

God every day you haven't had kids. Although I am surprised you haven't tried to trap my son for the rest of his life with a child. At least now he can still get a divorce and find a good woman to take care of him before I'm gone."

Okay, that was enough. I had been in that house for less than an hour and she was already pushing me too far. If we were going to make it in the same house together until Christmas, I needed to make a few things clear.

I stood up and stormed across the kitchen to where she was by the stove. "I'm only going to say this once, Varla." I'm not sure if it was the fury in my eyes or the tone of my voice, but she stepped away until her back hit the counter. Our faces were only inches apart, but I didn't care. She was going to hear everything I had to say even if it meant I had to hold her ass down and force her to listen.

"I'm not here for you. I'm here for Mark. I've put up with all your bullshit over the years for him, and let me tell you, I've had enough. I won't let you disrespect me like this anymore. It's time you started treating me like your son's wife instead of someone who's in the way of your relationship. I'm not trying to take him away from you, Varla. But you're doing a pretty damn good job of pushing him out of your life."

Varla waved a dismissive hand. "He'll always come back to me. He always does when his flings don't work out. I'm his mother and he needs me."

"A fling?" I laughed. A fling didn't last three years. "You're wrong. Mark is a grown man. He's fully capable of taking care of himself and choosing who he wants to spend the rest of his life with. He doesn't need your help. I suggest you get that through your head before he comes, or you may never see him again. Mark and I both agreed that this was the last straw with you. If you never want to see your son again, then keep treating me like shit and you'll get your wish."

Along with the shock at what I'd said, pain flickered across Varla's face. For the first time, it looked like I'd knocked her guard down and she was vulnerable.

The lid on the pot of stew bounced as the liquid bubbled beneath it. The hot stovetop sizzled when small drops splashed out and hit the surface, snapping Varla out of her momentary weakness.

She rushed to turn the burner off, but I was no longer hungry. I felt sick to my stomach for what I'd said to her, even if she did deserve every word. She was Mark's mother and this extra time was supposed to help us past our differences, not make our relationship worse. Besides, I really hated fighting with anyone. Varla brought out the worst in me and I allowed her to because I didn't control my temper.

"Varla, I…"

She put her hand up, but kept her eyes on the boiling liquid in the pot. "Don't worry about it. Everything will be fine by the time Mark arrives." Her voice was calm with no hint of the animosity I'd seen from the moment I knocked on the door.

Since I no longer felt like eating, I decided to get a good night sleep and start fresh with her in the morning. "Thank you for making this meal, but I think I'm going to turn in. I'm exhausted." I was, too. It had been an emotional day. Anxiety and anger could really drain a person.

Varla still didn't face me. "Fine. I'll see you in the morning."

I went back to the room that never changed, where I flopped down on the bed, and debated whether I should call Mark. I wanted to hear his voice. Plus, I didn't want him to find out from Varla that I told her this visit was her last chance to have Mark in her life. But if I called and told him about the argument, he'd only worry all night. Just because my night was ruined, it didn't mean I had to stress him out.

In the end, I decided on a hot shower and bed.

* * *

Cool fingers pressed into my wrist, causing me to wake with a start. I tried to sit up, but my hands and feet were bound to the bed.

"Shhh!" someone said from the darkness.

I squinted to try to make out a figure but the room was pitch black. I tugged against the restraints, but they didn't budge. My heart raced as I thought about the many reasons why I could be tied up in a bed in the middle of the night—someone broke in to steal, rape me, or even worse, kill me. And what had happened to Varla? She wouldn't have allowed someone to take her belongings or laid there and let them rape her. Varla would have fought back. Was she dead down the hall, or had they not found her yet? I had to think positive. Maybe they hadn't found her yet and I could distract them. Even if I didn't get along with the woman, if she woke up to the sound of me being raped, she'd call 9-1-1. She'd do something to help me. I had to believe that or I'd never get through this.

"What do you want?" I asked, my voice no more than a whisper. But I had to muster up more courage than that if I was going to wake up Varla. "I'll do whatever you want. Just tell me what to do?" I talked much louder that time.

Laughter followed my question.

"Please!" I begged. "I'll do anything."

"Anything but leave my son alone," Varla snapped.

I gasped. "Varla, is that you?" I couldn't believe it was her voice.

"Oh, don't act so surprised. Did you really think I wanted you to come all this way by yourself so we could bond?" She laughed again. "You're just as stupid as I thought you were."

"Varla, listen to me. If you let me go, I won't tell Mark. He won't have to know anything."

The lamp next to the bed came on, blinding me and causing my head to throb. I winced.

Varla stood over me in a white nightgown. "Head hurt?" she asked. "Don't worry, it'll pass. That's only from the sleeping aid I had to give you so you wouldn't wake up before I was ready for you to. It's a good thing you're a sound sleeper or I'd never have been able to give you a shot without you waking up."

"Why would you do this to me?" I always knew Varla was a horrible woman, but I'd never have guessed that she'd go so far as to kidnap me. How in the hell could she have given me a shot without my knowledge? Was I really sleeping that heavy? That was a scary thought, but I'd have to file it away for later. I had greater threats to deal with at the moment.

She sat on the bed next to me and brushed the hair off my face. "Maddy, did you honestly believe I'd let you take my son from me? He's my child and I've put up with you in the way long enough."

I squirmed against the restraints. Even now, she couldn't see that she was the one pushing Mark away. "Do you think Mark will come running with his arms wide open to you if he finds out you did this to me?"

Pity filled her eyes as she stared down at me. "Honey, he practically begged me to help him out of the relationship. As any good mother would do, I decided I'd give him what he wants for Christmas."

Every fiber of my being wanted not to believe her. Mark was my husband. But he must have given her some kind of signal that he wasn't completely happy in our relationship, or she wouldn't have me strapped to a bed in her house with the intent to rid me from his life. The pain of that was too much to bear. A tear rolled down my cheek before I could stop myself from crying in front of Varla.

She wiped it away. "Aww, look at that. You know I'm right."

"I don't." I argued because that seemed easier than accepting that my husband didn't want me around. "I want to hear Mark tell me he's not happy with me."

"I'm afraid talking to Mark isn't an option. It would ruin the surprise." She pulled a syringe out of the nightstand drawer. "It's time to get started if I'm going to have everything ready before he comes. It takes a lot of work to make someone vanish."

I squirmed as she brought the needle closer to my thigh. "Varla, don't do this! We can work something out!"

She smiled, jabbed the needle into my thigh, and plunged whatever was in the syringe into me. It didn't take long to take effect. My head swam, my vision blurred, and my eyelids drooped.

"That's right, don't fight it. When you wake up, you'll be in a different place."

"No," I slurred.

Everything went black.

* * *

I regained consciousness slowly. I could hear, smell, and feel long before I could move, talk, or open my eyes. For what seemed like hours, all I knew was that I was in a cold damp place with the scent of a rotten dead skunk in the air. A landfill? I couldn't be sure, but I didn't think I was in Varla's house anymore; I couldn't open my eyes to see.

For a long time, I lay on the damp, hard ground, willing myself to move until I finally managed to move one finger. Then, I focused on that one movement, wiggling it back and forth, until it spread into my hands, arms, and throughout my body. I had to restrain myself from a complete breakdown when I was able to open my eyes.

I stared up at the wooden rafters above me. I made out the initials MG carved in one of them. Not a landfill, but Varla's basement. I sat up fast, on alert. The basement was poorly lit by a single bulb in the laundry room behind a yellow curtain.

"Varla," I whispered. If she wasn't with me, I didn't want her to know I was awake yet. I had to think of a way to escape.

A low growl echoed through the small space. Flashes of Varla in her torn dress came to my mind.

I scrambled to my feet.

Chains rattled and a snarl ripped through the air.

I frantically scanned the area around me. The small light only illuminated the center of the room. The darkness still claimed the corners and other rooms of the basement. I took a step to the left, keeping my back against the wall, so I could see beyond the load-bearing post to the stairs. The path from where I stood was clear. If I ran, I might have been able to make it to the top before whatever Varla held captive caught me.

I closed my eyes, took two deep breaths to steady my nerves, and darted for the stairs.

But before I was halfway there, something gripped tight around both my ankles, and I was yanked off my feet, to send me face first to the floor. I didn't even have time to brace myself with my hands before smacking my nose into the hard concrete, which caused a very disturbing crunching sound. Blood oozed out of my nose. I spit as it went into my mouth. But I didn't have time to think about the pain or the blood. The other guest in the basement snarled and thrashed around, rattling chains. Whoever it was sounded like he might be in pain, too, or ready to attack. Either way, I didn't want to find out.

I couldn't believe I'd been so stupid as to think Varla had tossed me in the basement without insurance that I couldn't leave. If I'd thought before I ran, I might have noticed the clamps around my ankles that had chained me to the wall. The stairs were out of my reach and so was help.

The door opened on the first floor and a small amount of light flowed down the stairs. "What's going on down there?" Varla came halfway down and glared at me. She no longer had on her nightgown. She was dressed for the day in a t-shirt and jeans. Her hair was pulled up in a perfect bun on the top of her head. "Looks like you've made a mess of yourself."

"I need a doctor," I said. "I broke my nose. Please, just let me out. I'll tell them I fell down the stairs. I won't mention any of this." Of course, I would go right to the police and have her crazy ass committed, but that information wouldn't help me at the moment.

Varla waved a dismissive hand. "A little broken nose won't hurt my plans."

"You can't keep me down here forever. Mark will be here soon."

"You'll be gone before he shows up." She came down the rest of the stairs and stalked toward me. She gripped my chin between her thumb and fingers, yanking my head up so she could get a better look at my nose.

I swatted her hand away. "Don't touch me."

She cocked back her arm and backhanded me right in the nose.

I screamed and my natural instincts to defend myself kicked in. I grabbed hold of her bun and bounced her head off the stone wall.

When she hit the floor, I climbed on top of her, pinning her under me. "You're going to let me out of here," I said.

"You stupid girl," Varla snapped. "I'm done playing with you." She bucked under me until she freed her arm. With another hit to my broken nose, she tossed me off and slipped out of my reach. She was stronger than I thought.

Breathless, I sat on the floor holding my nose. My eyes were watering.

Varla adjusted her clothes and patted her now messy bun. "I can see you're not going to cooperate with me, so I'll need to speed things along. I did hope to have a little more time though."

I had to stall. If I could buy a little more time, I might have a chance to escape and call Mark. "What exactly do you plan to do with me?" I asked, not really wanting to know, but talking was better than letting her do anything rash.

She pulled the short pull cord on the light in the center of the basement. "You'll see exactly what I'm going to do with you." She walked over to the ugly yellow curtain that separated the laundry room and the main section of the basement.

The horror behind the curtain had me stumbling away until my back hit the wall. "W…what have you done?" I stammered, tears stinging my eyes when I saw the other person Varla had chained up in her basement.

Even with the black pillow case over his head, I recognized Frank Grimes by his favorite black and green flannel shirt that he wore over every t-shirt he owned, whether it matched or not. My heart ached to see the man who'd always been so nice to me with chains around his neck, feet, and wrists. But the bloodstains on his jeans that covered most of his left leg was what brought me to tears. He was hurt, and by the looks of his clothes, badly in need of medical attention.

The faint sound of the phone ringing had Varla glancing to the stairs. "That's probably Mark again. He's called three times looking for you. I told him you went to the store for his gift." A wicked smile spread across her face. "I can't ruin the surprise yet." She sounded so thrilled with herself for not spilling her plans to Mark. Even if Mark wanted nothing to do with me, I knew he wouldn't approve of the sick gift his mom had planned for Christmas.

"You should tell him now. Maybe he'll come early to see you." I was hoping to trick her into getting help for Frank and me.

She shook her head. "Not yet. Christmas will be here before we know it. Mark can wait for a couple of days."

I didn't really think that would work anyway, but I needed to keep her away from the phone. If Mark didn't hear from either of us for a lengthy period, he'd come.

"What do you plan to tell Mark when he shows up and I'm gone?" It was an effort to stall long enough for Mark to hang up.

She waved a dismissive hand. "Those are details you don't need to concern yourself with." Varla headed for the stairs as the phone kept ringing.

I prayed Mark would hang up.

"If you answer the phone, I'll scream as loud as I can," I threatened.

Varla didn't even pause. She knew Mark wouldn't be able to hear me, and even if he did, he would never be able to make out the words. Varla could tell him she was watching TV and he would believe her.

The basement door slammed and a moment later, I could hear Varla pick up the phone. Her voice was too low for me to hear anything after she said, "Hello."

I sighed and turned my attention to Frank. His head thrashed from side to side, as though he was trying to break free from the pillowcase. I scanned the basement for anything I could use to pick the lock on my chain to help him.

"Don't worry, Frank, I'm going to get us out of here."

Frank growled in response to my words and thrashed harder. My heart ached. He must be in such agony that he couldn't even form coherent words. I shuddered at the thought of what Varla, his own wife, had done to put him in that state, because she was about to do the same to me.

I stood up and walked until the restraints tightened around my ankle. There had to be something in the basement I could use as a weapon. When Varla returned, I could attack her and take the keys from her—I hoped she had them with her of course. Then while she was down, I would lock her ass up so she couldn't stop me from taking Frank and escaping.

I scanned the area around me that was within my reach.

Frank grew more anxious the closer I moved to him. I still wasn't anywhere near enough to touch him, but he pulled and yanked on his chains hard enough that I could have sworn I heard a crack. A moment later, one of the chains clattered to the floor loudly.

I glanced at the chain on the floor and my mouth dropped open. Frank's hand lay next to it on the concrete. He didn't even seem to notice the missing appendage. He didn't cry out in pain, or pause in his relentless attempts to escape. Blood dripped slowly from the nub where his hand used to be. Not at all as much blood as I thought would come from a wound like that. At least I knew he wouldn't bleed to death before I could help him. But first, I had to find a way to free myself, then I could save him.

Since there was nothing I could do for Frank from where I was, I went back to my search. There had to be something Varla had left behind. She couldn't have taken every last little thing out of the basement.

To my surprise, I didn't have to search long. "Thank God," I breathed. I had to force myself not to shout with joy when I saw one of Varla's hairpins on the floor.

I hurried over to grab it, but my leash stopped me only a few feet away. I wasn't about to give up, though. I got down on my hands and knees and crawled until my chains were as tight as I could stand them. Then, I stretched out on my belly until my fingertips gripped the small pin.

When the basement door opened and Varla stormed down the stairs, I scrambled to return to my spot by the wall, holding the pin in my hand.

"What are you doing?"

"Nothing," I answered a little too hastily.

Varla narrowed her eyes at me. "You expect me to believe that? I think I need to finish our conversation before you get any more bright ideas." She walked over to Frank. "What did you do to him?" She almost shouted at me as she examined Frank's bleeding wound.

"He did that to himself."

Without taking her eyes off Frank, she said, "He wouldn't hurt himself like this. You had to have done something to him."

"I'm all the way over here, Varla. How do you think I did that from here?"

Her gaze moved slowly from Frank to me. "Then you must have provoked him." She took a small silver key out of her pocket and unlocked the chain around Frank's neck, then she yanked the pillowcase off.

I gasped. Frank's pale face made the dark circles under his eyes almost look black and blue. The gash on his head oozed a green liquid down the right side of his face, but that wasn't the most startling thing about his appearance. The whites of his eyes were now a bloody red and the irises were a grayish white; he was missing teeth, too.

Varla laughed at my horrified expression. "Frank did die. But to my surprise, he woke up a couple of hours later. Luckily for him, I was so overwhelmed with grief that I hadn't called an ambulance yet. I did, however, call Mark and tell him his father had just died."

"You're lying." No way in hell did Frank die and come back to life. Varla must have done something to him. There was a rational explanation for his eyes. He was older, cataracts was a good possibility.

Frank snapped what little teeth he had left at Varla, who just smiled at him. "Don't worry, honey, I'll feed you soon," she said, but he didn't settle down. Instead, her voice only made him thrash against the chains and snarl at her. She turned her attention back to me. "It's a miracle he's still here. God sent him to me so I could remove you from my son's life easily. God wants me to get rid of you, Maddy. It's his way of handing me the perfect Christmas present for Mark. He deals with people so much better than I ever could. He's made to dispose of people. No one will ever know you didn't come back from your fake shopping trip. As far as Mark will know, he'll believe you ran off with another man and won't ever hear from you again. I'll get my family back, and Frank will be picking you out of his teeth for a week."

I was in utter shock. Somehow she'd turned into a religious nut at the moment in her life when she'd chosen to sin in a big way. How did she not see how fucked up that was? Did she think that she could simply chop me up and fry me for her husband? Frank would know if she did. He wouldn't actually make a meal out of me. The thought made my stomach twist uneasily. No person in their right mind would eat another human being if they didn't have to…but…Frank was in a horrible situation. I couldn't say what he would do to make his wife release him from this hell.

"You're crazy." I said, not sure what else to say to her. She was on a completely different level of crazy that I didn't even begin to understand. I was unarmed when it came to dealing with a psychotic nut job.

Varla laughed. "Thank you, dear." She replied as if I'd just paid her the greatest of complements. "Now, I'm going to finish up a few details before we can get started. To insure you won't try anything stupid, I think I'll loosen the chains around Frank. He'll keep you in line." I hadn't noticed before that Frank's chains were attached to a pulley above his head. The one around his neck, wrists, and ankles all came together and were attached to a longer chain that Varla could adjust.

The minute Frank had a little wiggle room, Varla dashed halfway up the stairs and out of his reach. Frank didn't move. He hadn't noticed she'd given him more room to roam until she said, "Don't have too much fun while I'm away. I wouldn't want to miss the show," and hurried up the stairs and slammed the door. I heard the lock click in place a second later.

Frank seemed to respond to her voice and he jerked his arms; this time he wasn't held back.

With slow, stiff movements, he shuffled toward me. Baring his rotting teeth at me, he snarled, reminding me of something I'd see an animal do while stalking their prey before pouncing. His shoulders were hunched, but his eyes were wide and fixated on me.

"Frank, it's me. Maddy. You don't want to hurt me. I'll help you out of here." I tried to reason with him.

He let out a bloodcurdling howl that sounded like a rabid dog and lunged at me. Fortunately, the chains tightened and he landed inches away from my feet.

I flinched and pulled my knees to my chest, trying to keep every inch of my body out of his reach. Even if I didn't believe that Frank had died and returned to life, I knew something horrible had happened to him. He wasn't himself, and I had no clue what he was capable of. His chains rattled as he struggled to reach me. I had to escape, and fast.

Keeping as close to the wall as possible, I held up the hairpin.

Frank moved slowly. He groaned as he struggled to get back on his feet. Every joint in his body seemed to lock up when he tried to bend or unbend. It was sad to watch. His body didn't seem to want to follow instructions from his brain, but after several tries, he managed to get back on his feet.

The murderous expression he aimed at me pinned me where I stood. I could see in his expression that he meant to hurt me at any cost, no matter what I did or said. Varla's threat of him eating me no longer seemed like a false story. He snapped his remaining teeth and growled ferociously at me.

My hands trembled as I tried to get the pin in the small key hole of the lock on my restraints. I'd never picked a lock before. I wished it hadn't taken me being a prisoner to need to figure it out. I jabbed the small pin in the lock and twisted it back and forth, yanking on it each time. It wouldn't open.

"Damn it. Come on," I scolded myself, trying to steady my hands. It always looked so easy in movies. Why couldn't I pick a simple padlock? It wasn't rocket science. Even the stupidest criminals could pick a lock in a matter of seconds, yet though I was in mortal danger, I couldn't free myself.

I tried again and again. I tried different angles, pushed the pin in deeper, applied more pressure, less pressure, then twisted harder. Then I bent the damn pin and managed to get it stuck in the hole. Tears welled in my eyes as defeat coursed through me.

I'd broken the one thing that might have helped me escape, and managed to make sure the key wouldn't work all at the same time.

Frustrated, I beat the lock on the floor, which only jammed the pin inside farther. To my astonishment, the lock clicked open. I laughed almost hysterically. Guess I'd been going about it the hard way. I quickly freed myself.

I'd been so focused on my task, I hadn't noticed that Frank was still thrashing around, trying his damndest to get to me. With a quick glance at the pin stuck in the lock, I knew I'd never be able to use it to free Frank, too. I would have to deal with my mother-in-law and take the key from her. I went for the stairs.

Frank snapped his remaining teeth and snarled. His eyes narrowed and he crouched down, ready to attack the minute I was in reach.

I backed up a couple of steps. "Frank, I need to go by you. I'll bring you help, but you have to let me go upstairs."

He rattled his chains around his remaining arm and legs. His handless arm flailed around in the air at me. I kept going, telling myself he wouldn't hurt me. Varla had to be lying, because people didn't come back to life once they died. Whatever was wrong with him, the Frank I knew was still in there and I hoped I could reason with him.

"Frank, it's Maddy. I need your help so we can get out of here." I kept my voice low and soft. I wanted him to hear all the fear I felt.

A low rumble built in his chest before a vicious growl ripped through the air. The sound was so horrific that every hair on my body stood on end, but I closed the distance between us. The longer I wasted time, the more of a chance I had of Varla catching me.

Frank reached out with his only hand and grabbed a handful of my shirt. He pulled me close to him. That's when I smelled the awful stench coming off him. He smelled like rotten, dead skunk. But I didn't have time to think about it. His mouth was inches away from my face. Varla wasn't lying; he was trying to munch on me.

I yanked free and stumbled back out of his reach. That's when I finally took a good look at him. I'd only seen him as my father-in-law who was injured by his wife before. But now that I was close enough, I really took a good look at him. His skin was discolored, almost purplish. Some spots appeared to be flaking off. The inside of his mouth was black. Dead tissue, I thought, horrified.

"Impossible," I muttered, but couldn't stop myself from moving closer to him. I snagged his arm still with a hand and held tight. He fought against me so I squeezed tighter.

Like a sleeve, Frank's skin peeled down under my fingers as he slid his arm out of my grip. It made the most disgusting suction sound I had ever heard. His skin literally felt like jello in my hand.

Shocked, sick, and confused, I stared at the flesh and blood on my fingers. This wasn't possible. Everything I'd learned in my entire life said that when you died, you were gone for good. You didn't wake up and become a prisoner in the home you lived in. You didn't try to eat the people you loved. You went in the ground and your family missed you until you were reunited in whatever afterlife you believed in. This wasn't right, but he was dead. He wouldn't just let me stroll up the stairs. But how did you hurt someone who wasn't alive? Hell, he'd probably just jump back up if I tried to kill him.

The only option I had was to bring my mother-in-law back down, attack her, and leave her to be the distraction so I could escape. It didn't break my heart to take out the woman who had captured me and intended to kill me as a Christmas present for her son.

"Varla!" I shouted, not giving myself time to back out. Even though my heart pounded in my chest, I forced myself to stay on guard. Varla was strong. I'd figured that out during our fight. She wasn't about to go down easy and it was going to be difficult to get her to willingly enter the basement with Frank on such a long leash.

Footsteps stomped across the floor above me as Varla made her way to the basement door. She'd heard me. The door creaked open and she came down halfway, only enough to see me.

"What?" she snapped.

Now I had to think of something to get her to come down. I glanced around the cellar. "Frank's hurt," I blurted out.

She narrowed her eyes at me, but scrutinized every inch of Frank that she could see from her perch on the stairs.

"His arm's peeling off," I added. "I think he's decomposing. He won't last much longer unless you wrap it up to stop the decay." I bit my lip, hoping she wouldn't call bullshit on my lie.

She stared at Frank for a second longer before sighing and stalking back upstairs.

My heart sank. I'd used the one thing I didn't believe Varla could refuse, but she had walked away, like losing Frank was nothing. He was the key to her entire twisted plan. I didn't understand how she could just leave him like that, not that she could do anything for him. If he was dead, his body would continue to rot no matter what she did. But I wasn't about to tell her that.

I was just about to take my chances with Frank, now that I knew he was damageable, when Varla appeared on the staircase again. She held a bloody, round steak in her left hand. She dangled it in front of her.

Frank's gaze automatically went to her, all of his attention now focused on Varla's hand. He let out a low growl, but the sound didn't make me cringe. He didn't sound violent, but relieved to see her with some food.

She stalked down the stairs and walked right up to her husband. He tried to snatch the steak out of her hand, but she yanked it back at the last minute. Slowly, and deliberately, Varla pushed him back to the wall he'd been chained against when I first saw him. Once she had him in place, she let him have the steak and rushed to tighten the chains. Then she dug in her pockets and pulled out various sizes of Band-Aids and gauze. I waited until she had her back to me and fully focused on the job at hand, then I lunged at her.

I had no weapon, only the element of surprise, and boy was Varla surprised when I knocked her to the floor. Her eyes bugged and her mouth fell open. I would enjoy the memory of her shocked expression later, but for now, I had to get her restrained.

She wiggled under me, bucking like she had before, but I was ready for it this time. I held firm and stayed on her. I had to be quick, though; Frank was almost done with his steak, and we would be his next meal. I for one, didn't have any desire to be chomped on. I wished for a weapon to threaten Varla with, as she would never willingly let me lock her up.

So I figured I would just have to knock her silly first and make her cooperate. I grabbed a handful of her hair and bounced her head off the floor a couple of times. Not hard enough to give her brain damage, only enough to stun her.

Frank finished his meal and glanced at the two of us with hunger in his eyes. He bared his rotten teeth and crouched down. I grabbed Varla and moved, forgetting that Frank's leash wasn't as long as before. He couldn't get to me or Varla, but that didn't stop him from trying.

"Get off me!" Varla snapped and delivered a blow to the side of my head that made spots appear in my vision.

I quickly shook it off and returned the favor. "This can go easy, or not. But I will get out of here," I told her.

"No, you won't," Varla hissed and hit me again. She knocked me sideways enough to buck me off her. I should have bashed her head in at my first opportunity.

Varla stood over me. I pretended to be scared and stayed where I was. Just as I knew she would, Varla came over and tried to kick me. Instead, I grabbed her ankle and delivered a kick of my own, right into her stomach. She flew backwards, landing at Frank's feet.

"You stupid bitch!" she shouted breathlessly, and hurried out of Frank's reach before standing again. She wasn't about to let me go easily. I had to take her down and that was the problem. I'd wanted nothing more than to go free, but I couldn't seem to kill her. I could chain her up and bring the police, but I wouldn't steal her life away from her. If Mark did still love me, he wouldn't look too kindly on me taking his mother away from him. He wouldn't understand unless he had proof. I had to get out alive, and leave Varla breathing when I did.

She moved toward me. "I'm going to enjoy killing you. But I think I'll take my time and watch you suffer first."

I laughed. "Because the rest of this has been such a pleasure."

"I went easy on you before. I tried to do this nicely, but you're making things so much harder on us both. Now I think I'll wrap your head up and give it to Mark on Christmas morning. I'll let him know what an evil bitch you truly are."

The murderous rage that coursed through me made me rethink the idea of leaving her alive. I'd kill her fast and get the hell out of there. She was sick and didn't deserve to spread her illness to anyone else. "Come and get me," I gestured with my middle finger in a come here motion.

She just chuckled at me. "Do you think I'm that stupid? I can see you think I've lost my mind, but I've never thought so clearly in my life. This is what God wanted. I'm not going to fail him when he controls my afterlife." She went to Frank's chains and lengthened the leash again. "I'll come back once you've calmed down. If Frank has a meal of you before I do, well, I guess he'll save me the trouble of dealing with the mess." She headed for the stairs.

I glanced at Frank for a split second, and decided the risk was worth it. I darted toward her, snagging Varla by the back of the shirt before she even made it up two of the stairs. That was the good news. The bad news was that Frank had also caught me with his mangled hand. Fear ran through me at his icy touch. I hadn't noticed how cold he was before.

Varla fought against me as Frank tried his hardest to keep hold of me. His teeth snapped and he growled, but I wouldn't be his meal just yet. I mustered up all the strength I had, gripped Varla tighter, and yanked her back. The fear in her eyes when she landed against Frank gave me a sick satisfaction.

I dashed up the stairs, but I only made it to the third one before Varla grasped my ankle and yanked my feet out from under me. I smacked my chin on a step, biting my tongue. Blood pooled in my mouth.

"Not so fast," Varla hissed.

I rolled and kicked with all my might. My foot landed squarely in her belly, sending her backwards. She fell to the floor at Frank's feet. He let out a ferocious snarl and lunged at her, tossing his entire body on top of her. Varla struggled beneath him, but her efforts were useless. Frank sank his teeth into her throat.

"Frank!" Varla cried out, but he didn't even flinch.

He ripped a chunk of flesh from her neck and chewed on it like it was the world's finest T-bone steak. Blood squirted from her throat like a faucet. She put a hand over the wound, but the blood continued to shoot out between her fingers. The slab of flesh was gone in an instant; I wasn't even sure Frank had chewed. Then he dove back down and snagged another bite, this time off her face, exposing her cheekbone.

She let out another cry. "Maddy, don't…leave…me…down here." She gasped and coughed up blood.

I no longer saw the need to keep her alive. I felt nothing for her at all. The gruesome scene in front of me made my stomach lurch, but nausea was all the feelings I had for the situation unfolding before me.

"Goodbye, Varla. I hope you rot in Hell." I turned and walked up the stairs.

When I reached the first floor, I saw that Varla had been busy since she'd locked me in the basement. Christmas decorations hung from everything, soft music played in the background, and the kitchen table was full of wrapped presents. One of them only had wrapping paper on half of it. I went to investigate.

The large box on the table, with only one-half of it covered in snowmen wrapping paper, made me laugh. Varla really was a crazy bitch. I glanced at the basement door. Now I could really call her my monster-in-law, or zombie-in-law—whatever worked. But the box before me took the cake. The box was marked, 'Choice meats.' It was a goddamned steak package. The tag sitting beside it had Frank's name on it. Several of the other presents on the table had his name on them, too. One had Mark's.

I knew it was stupid, but I was curious. Who would know? I ripped the paper off, and tossed it to the floor and gasped. In marker she'd written on the box, "To my son who will stay with me forever, just like his father." It was another box of meat. So she had planned to turn him into one of those monsters just so she didn't have to lose him. Crazy didn't even begin to cover her.

Frank groaned loudly. His cry echoed up the stairs. His meal was gone. Varla wasn't coming after me. I was free to leave this hellhole.

Varla thought she was going to give Mark the best Christmas present of all, but in the end, it was me instead who would give him the best present. Mark wouldn't become the monster Varla had wanted him to, and he would never know about any of what had occurred.

I turned the gas on the stove, and before the house filled with the flammable fumes, I grabbed a lighter out of the kitchen drawer, and began making a trail of fire to the front door. I ignited the curtains in the living room, Varla's ugly yellow and brown throw-blanket on the back of her couch, and the presents under the tree.

Flames crackled and licked up the tree and the walls in a matter of minutes. I stood and watched for a second, making sure it wouldn't go out.

When I was positive the flames were strong, I walked through the front door without another glance at the house of horrors.

I could face whatever came next with Mark. At least I knew he was safe, and so was I.

# GREEN CHRISTMAS

TONY GARCIA

1

Karl Morgan was a rancher from a long family of farmers and ranchers. Their ranch in Rutherford was Karl's favorite thing in or about California. Generations of Morgans were born, raised, and worked on that ranch. Now Karl was the last; ever since his wife passed a few years back and his youngest daughter had grown up and moved away. So many memories flooded those walls, so many laughs, so many tears, and more holidays than Karl could try to remember. Christmas was his favorite out of all of them. Not just the day itself, but the season. People just seemed a little bit nicer to each other during that time. Maybe it was the exhilarating chill in the morning air, or the hot cocoa, or maybe the glow of a fireplace that welcomed people home after a long day. Whatever the reason, Karl loved it.

Driving his old '62 Chevy pickup truck through the back roads and over the hills just in time to greet the sunrise was an old habit of Karl's. Twice each week Karl drove past the trees and vineyards, loving every minute of the Napa Valley on his way into town for breakfast.

"Yes, sir. This is perfect weather." Karl rolled down his window and then turned on the radio, tuning it until he found a station playing Christmas songs. Without thinking, he found himself singing along and tapping his fingers on the steering wheel. It was more dumb luck than reflexes that caused Karl to slam on his brakes a moment later.

Near the crest of the hill a dark gray van sat parked, nearly invisible in the coming dawn. Once Karl had regained his wits, he looked about for the driver.

"Maybe they broke down. Hell of a place to have motor problems." Living alone over the years, Karl had taken to talking to himself quite a bit. Opening the driver's door, he swung his six foot, two hundred and eighty pound frame out of the pickup, straightened his overalls, and made his way towards the van. He stopped near the rear truck bed just long enough to stretch his back and scratch his great beard with a huge morning yawn.

"Hello! Y'all okay over there?"

As if on cue, a much smaller nondescript man ran in a scrambling panic from the edge and jumped into the van. Without a word, the van sped off over the hill, leaving Karl standing in mid-stretch like a great old bear.

"Well now. That's peculiar." Karl rubbed his beard and stared after the fleeting taillights of the van as it crested the hilltop and vanished from sight. "Right damn peculiar." Curiosity urged him forward. Squinting against the rising sun, he scanned down the moss and leaf-covered ridgeline, hoping to see what had spooked the driver. After a few minutes, he spotted a curving trail of crushed grass leading down the hill. With a heavy sigh—and another great stretch of his back—Karl began slowly and carefully following the weaving trail. "Yes, sir, damn peculiar, indeed."

At the base of the hill was a creek of flowing water. "Ew-wee, it sure didn't look that far from the road." He wiped his brow and once again gave his back a stretch. In the middle of the creek, about twenty yards from the edge, sat two large metal barrels, both capsized and both cracked open. Green ooze pored from the cracks to mix with the stream. Karl rubbed his beard and contemplated the surroundings. "Well, them barrels is too big for me to haul out by myself. No-siree, Karl, you ain't the man you once was." Looking west, then south, Karl knew what he had to do. "Ah best go warn them weird kids that live downstream." Another stretch and he began huffing his way back up the knoll, murmuring along the way. "Wouldn't want their crops to get ruined on account of some corroded barrels and such. 'Specially since all them weird kids eat is greens. No, sir, wouldn't be right just to ignore such a thing as damn peculiar as this."

2

Oswald the rooster crowed at the first rays of light. He wondered, as he often did, why he was the only creature smart enough to greet the sun each new day. Sure, the humans who relied on his dedication eventually arose and conducted their far less important tasks about the farm, but none of them fathomed the perfection of the morning sun. At least they fed him well; if only they would branch out and bring him a chick or two, the rest of his day wouldn't be nearly as dull.

Little did Oswald know, but many of the humans were already awake and greeting the sun in their own way.

For them, life was indeed grand in their Vegan commune, hidden deep within the Napa Valley. It was hard to believe that only a short few years ago, six couples—all friends from college—had decided to strike out on their own and create a utopia. Positive more would follow their ideal, they bought a plot and tilled the land. 'Nature will provide' was their credo, and they swore only to farm the land naturally, nurturing the earth for its bounty, while preserving its integrity. Slowly, over the past few years they had grown from a few tents to brick buildings—brick they made themselves from the mud and rocks in the area.

Jan and Fred had hatched the original idea one morning over a *soy latte*. Rich, Sue, Jeff, and Tina had jumped in immediately. Others, such as Gina, Salina, Gerald, Thelma, Bruce, and Jerome had joined the group later. Each provided their own dynamic idiom to the equation. They farmed what they needed and any excess was traded weekly at the Farmer's Market. Peaceful within their paradise, they wanted for nothing; content in the truth that their lives would never change.

Jeff and Tina were already up and enjoying a brisk cup of herbal tea while they watched the sunrise. Smiling stupidly at each other, as young lovers often did, they grooved to *Ekoostik Hookah* until the rays of sunlight peered into their bedroom. Then Jeff unfolded from Tina's loving arms to make breakfast. He was a renaissance man after all, and just because he enjoyed cooking and was slightly on the effeminate side, did not mean that he was any less of a man.

Minutes later, adding fresh parsley from his personal garden, he stirred the tofu into a semblance of scrambled eggs while Tina smiled and sipped her tea, satisfied with the knowledge that Jeff was hers to command.

Across the compound and through the trees, Gerald languished in the water, swimming to the bottom, drinking in Nature's finest, and frolicking like a child when no one was looking. Life was great! Gerald was usually the first person up and he loved to bathe under the last remnants of night, just as the light of day began to shine through the trees. It was a magical hour for him. The creek was always refreshing at this time of day, though today the current seemed a bit warmer than usual.

After his bath, Gerald strolled through the woods, stopping now and again to smell the flowers, breathe in the clean air, and reflect on the love of his life. Thelma was a gorgeous woman with blonde hair, blue eyes, and no matter where they were, Gerald knew that as long as they were together, it was home.

Suddenly, a wave of dizziness, bordering on nausea slapped him in the face and he found himself sitting in the grass, leaning against a great oak tree. Even being a Vegan was all right, as long as she was his. Scratching absently at a spot on his lower back, he decided he would have Thelma check him for poison ivy; at least it would be a great idea to get her naked. The itch moved to his shoulder blades and his original thoughts of sex faded into the dawning realization that his only physical contact for the immediate future would probably be Aloe leaves. Perhaps it was the thought of this that made his legs itch as well. "Great. Now I have a rash."

He suddenly realized just how much he was perspiring, which was very odd, considering the coolness of the morning air. Maybe he was getting sick. Perhaps his pattern of diving into cold water every morning had caught up with him in the form of a flu bug. The flowers around him blurred out of focus for a scant second and the ground threatened to reach up and grab him. "Just need a minute. Need to catch my breath." His body had gone from a profuse sweat to an extreme lack of perspiration in a matter of minutes. That alone was enough to cause a mild shock in anyone; at least that was how Gerald rationalized it.

The itching quickly turned to electric shocks of pain that ran through his entire body, and Gerald convulsed on the ground like a fish out of water. After a few moments of what felt like eternity, Gerald stopped moving and lay still on his back. His eyes slowly rolled skywards and took on a sickly yellow tinge, as his body released the last gasp of air it would ever know.

3

Never one to judge a person by their beliefs, no matter how crazy they might seem, Karl drove to the center of the commune. With a nod to the large rooster perched atop a signpost painted with a peace symbol, he turned off the engine and looked around for someone to warn within the half-dozen or so crude mud huts.

He was relieved when a young man walked out of a stone hut to the left. He hated the thought of waking someone over what was probably nothing; that would just be rude. A young woman followed slowly behind the young man, and then another couple approached from a similar hut to the right. They were each in their early twenties, skinny, a bit on the hairy side in Karl's personal opinion, and dressed mostly in what looked like burlap. It was almost as if pretty people had gone out of their way to make themselves less attractive.

"To each their own" Karl reminded himself. Donning his most winning smile, he waved and walked to greet the nearest young man. The young people greeted his warm smile with mixed expressions, ranging from cynicism to outright hostility. But try as he might, Karl simply couldn't follow the logic, or lack thereof, within the string of words they launched at him; as it could hardly be called a conversation. Questions mixed with accusations and ridiculous statements flew, seemingly at random in Karl's general vicinity, and he realized he wasn't prepared for the sheer amount of peculiarity this morning had to offer.

"Is there a problem?"

"Are you lost?"

"Did you know you're trespassing?" was blurted out so quickly from between two small young women, a blonde and a brunette, that Karl was unable to tell who had asked what first.

"Well, I..." he stammered.

"Let me guess! There's a problem with the Beef Baron's association!" This was followed by a cacophony of laughter.

"Uh, not that I'm rightly aware." Karl wondered if there was a Beef Baron's association.

"Perhaps you've come to regale us with fragments of knowledge, gained from years of exploiting our four-legged brethren!" Boos and hisses echoed the sentiment.

"Exploiting who...what..." What was wrong with these people, he wondered.

"Very eloquent, Farmer Bob. Your fundamental grasp of the English language is astounding!" someone chimed in with snickering added for effect.

"It's Karl, not Bob, actually, and I just came to tell..."

"What makes you think there's anything you can tell us? We're enlightened beyond the boundaries of flesh and your cycle of senseless death! What possible wisdom do you deign to bestow upon us, oh great carnivore?" a woman asked.

Stunned silence followed that particular tirade for a few seconds, and Karl wondered if perhaps no one else really knew what she was talking about either.

Karl squinted and stared at the diminutive woman standing in front of him; arms folded across her chest and a look of pure contempt rampant on her face. She reminded him of a small orphaned boy from a Charles Dickens' novel. His jaw nearly hit the ground when he recognized Janet and it nearly took his senses away with his breath. "Jan...um...okay...I was driving over yonder and..." He gestured with his thumb towards the highway, hoping this new train of thought would derail the old one, whatever it was.

"Yonder? Yonder? O-M-G who talks like that anymore?" one of the young men, chimed in amongst chuckles and more snickers.

"Yeah...and well..." Karl prided himself on his patience and acceptance of others, but even he had limits.

"Driving! So you're a murderer of animals and the planet!" Two of the more effeminate males shared a high-five, congratulating each other on their witticism.

"Whatever...look I saw this guy up on the hill..." Karl felt his anger rising steadily.

"This guy? And you just assumed he came from here? Well, you have a lot of..."

Karl had had enough! With emphasis, he pointed with his entire hand at the dirty waif in front of him to make it very clear he was done putting up with their nonsense.

"SHUT UP, YA DERN FOOL! Check your water!" Karl pointed through the trees and towards the creek. Without waiting for another bout of who knows what that was, Karl climbed into his pickup and drove away, taking a combination of bewilderment and frustration with him.

4

After a lengthy series of self-adulation, over their mental conquest of 'Crazy old Farmer Karl,' Jan, Fred, Rich, Sue, Bruce and Jerome returned to their respective huts to begin their days in earnest. Gina and Salina, as they did most mornings, had slept in, completely missing the excitement.

Jeff and Tina enjoyed their tea, while watching the scene unfold from the comfort of their hemp pajamas and the melodies of Addison Groove Project.

Thelma, meanwhile, finished making breakfast for Gerald and herself. Gerald liked to wake up early and sneak out of bed, to swim around naked when no one was looking. Thelma had followed him one morning, and had marveled how her love so resembled a forest spirit straight out of one of those books she should have read when she was younger, but she chose to see the movie instead. She neatly arranged the cereal, tea pot, and honey on the table, for the third time. Gerald was much later than usual.

A shuffle at the door must have meant he'd read her mind. Shuffle... stumble... shuffle. Odd, Gerald was normally quite graceful, she thought. He must have a surprise for her.

"Breakfast is ready and on the table," she called.

A shambling scrape from the other room was the only response.

"Gerald, quit playin' around. Get in here and eat." Again, her voice was met with a dragging shuffle, albeit closer than the last. Then, another closer shuffle, accompanied by a single word uttered by a voice that sounded like it was strained through gravel "*Brains...*"

"Yes, yes. I know; you love me for my brains. My second best asset, as you like to point out, mister." Thelma stifled a small giggle.

The horror that was once Gerald stood behind Thelma. His eyes were sunken, his features gaunt and jaundiced, with a small trail of yellow drool dribbling from his gaping maw, its only function, at present, was to form the word "*Brains...*"

"Okay, look, this just isn't funny anymore. You're being repetitive and stupid. Now..." Suddenly Thelma's cereal bowl was much closer than it had been a few seconds ago. This thought was preceded by the memory of a blunt trauma to the back of her skull, and shortly thereafter, a loud crunching noise and an intense pain, that faded into whatever it was she'd been feeling. In a sudden epiphany, she realized that her breakfast hadn't gotten any closer, it was just that her eyeball was now hanging directly over it. But that was absurd. After all, how could she see her own eyeball and not feel the pain?

Darkness claimed any possibility of another thought forming in Thelma's once pretty, but oh so vapid, and now blood-soaked head.

Gerald finished slurping pieces of Thelma's brain from her open skull like a dog at a food bowl. Now that her head was empty, for real, the hunger struck at him all over again. It pulled at him, gnawed at his every second; he needed to eat to stop the pain. Slowly, he rose and shambled to visit the neighbors.

* * *

Bruce whistled as he pulled vegetables from the garden and Jerome took them inside to wash. Their relationship had started in high school, but it was a secret until college and then, well, it really wasn't much of a secret or surprise to anyone who knew them.

Shaking loose dirt from a turnip, Bruce was surprised to see Gerald walking towards him. Standing, Bruce raised one arm to his forehead, in an attempt to block the glare of the morning sun. Gerald was normally inside with Thelma until later in the day, and it was even more of a shock when Gerald reached out to embrace Bruce. Gently, yet firmly, Bruce attempted to abate Gerald's advances.

"Gerald! I didn't know...I mean...we...can't..." The rest was a gurgle of gibberish. Blood gushed through the cavernous hole in Bruce's throat and he collapsed to the ground, dead before his knees ever touched dirt.

It was at this moment that Jerome exited the hut for his next batch of vegetables. He arrived in time to see his lover drop from Gerald's embrace to his knees, as if Bruce was kneeling before Gerald

"Hey!" Jerome dropped his basket and charged at the two men before his eyes told his brain about the abomination that stood before him, which curdled his blood to ice. Before Jerome could scream for help, the horror once known as Gerald was upon him; tearing, ripping, rending flesh from his face and throat. Gerald was covered in blood, bone, bits of skin, and other less recognizable gore. The corpses of Jerome and Bruce lay at hiss feet, and sensing there were no further distractions, Gerald set about the task of crushing their skulls in and devouring the smorgasbord of cerebellum and cerebrum before him.

But no matter how much he ate, the hunger gnashed at him, never abating, coursing pain through his animated cadaver form and driving him towards further acts of depravity.

Gina and Salina were next on Gerald's menu. They lay in bed, enjoying each other's sleepy embrace, completely oblivious of the morning's events, and content to keep it that way. Gerald's hunger decided otherwise and propelled him through their window directly on top of the lounging beauties. It would be senseless to describe them at this point, considering their entrails were torn from their bodies and used to decorate the walls, and their pretty faces were masticated into several pieces, to then be strewn around the small room. No amount of forensic fortitude could ever piece the remains of Gina or Salina together again.

Perhaps it was the crash of the window, or the brief, though excruciating, screams of horror that roused Rich and Sue to action. Had they heard the sounds of flesh being torn from arms, or marrow being sucked from thighs, their curiosity might never have been piqued. In fact, had they recognized either of those sounds, they may have been able to prepare themselves for the macabre scene that awaited them. Better yet, it may have given them enough sense to run like hell.

"Is everyone all right?" Rich asked to the interior as he opened the door and stepped inside the small hut. Oftentimes, his mind had hoped to catch the ladies in a compromising, and by that he meant sexual and nude, position. But what he saw this day was undoubtedly not what he had in mind. Gerald sat cross-legged, with his mouth buried inside the crevice that was Salina's head. Rich stood in shock, unknowing what to do next. The sight of Gerald sucking a stringy piece of brain between his teeth, much like a child eating spaghetti, was more than Rich could take. Vomiting uncontrollably all over the floor, walls, and his beloved red-headed Sue, was all the action Rich could muster. Sue, in turn retched profusely over any area that had not already been covered by her partner.

Not one to miss an opportunity in life, Gerald held true to his old instincts, even in death. Springing to as much life as a reanimated corpse can, Gerald was at the couple before they had a chance to react. Grabbing Rich by his face, Gerald slammed him into and through the coffee table, breaking his neck in two places. Newfound strength and energy flowed through dead Gerald. In fact, he was more powerful in death than he ever could have been in life, but this thought never occurred to him. This, like everything else, was blurred by the pain and the only way to get rid of the pain, was to eat. Unable to make a hasty escape, Sue became part of the bed frame, as Gerald split her body in twain across a bed post, with one almost casual toss over his shoulder.

The better part of the afternoon was spent devouring the couples, but still it wasn't enough. As dusk approached, the pain returned and Gerald was driven forward to find relief. From hut to hut he traveled, leaving carnage in his wake, until nearly every one of his friends were dead.

Only Jan and Fred remained.

5

It was about this time that Jan and Fred realized none of their friends had been around most of the day, and that something just might be amiss.

Ever the chivalrous one, Fred went first to Gina and Salina's hut, where it took everything he had not to scream in terror, lose bladder control, or vomit without end. His brain refused to absorb the entire scene, and he had no arguments with that particular self-defense mechanism. Rushing out of the hut, he was just in time to stop Jan from entering. He dragged her by the hand behind him, running for their home, ignoring her constant complaining and questioning along the way. Frantically, he ransacked their place until he found his axe. "Stay here!" his yell gave no chance for Jan to retort, and Fred bolted back towards the center of the commune, frantically hoping in vain that some of his friends were still alive, that what he'd witnessed was an isolated event.

Fred came across one dreadful scene after another, though, until he traced the devastation to Tina and Jeff's place. Upon arriving, he found the door was smashed inwards and the sounds of *10 Foot Ganja Plant* echoed within the remaining silence; a silence that was broken seconds later by the sounds of slurping and lip smacking.

Axe held in front of him, as armor and weapon, Fred cautiously entered the home of his friends. His mind was steeled for anything, or so he thought. Gerald was sitting at the table, scraping the inside of Tina's open skull with a wooden serving spoon like it was a pumpkin. For a brief second, it reminded Fred that Christmas was right around the corner and he had planned to make pies. Gerald stared blankly through the yellow orbs, set deep in his eye sockets, and Fred brandished the axe admonishingly.

"Gerald! How could you! You're a vegetarian!"

Gerald dropped Tina's carcass unceremoniously and shambled towards dessert. Fred, realizing the futility of words, and to be honest had never really liked Gerald anyway, swung the axe with all his might. Blade met muscle and cleaved through bone and sinew alike. Gerald's right arm flew away from his body, leaving a trail of thick yellow liquid in its wake. The axe became embedded deep in Gerald's ribcage. The force of the blow knocked Gerald backwards, wrenching the axe from Fred's trembling grasp as the body fell.

Unfortunately for Fred, the undead Gerald recovered much quicker than could be anticipated, and was atop Fred before he could find a replacement weapon. With one good hand, Gerald squeezed Fred's throat until his larynx imploded, then the zombie smashed Fred's cranium open on the corner of the table.

*"Brains..."*

Despite Fred's warning, Jan came inside to investigate after hearing all the noise. Reeling at the horror before her, Jan shrieked and ran out of the hut, dashing blindly into the nearby trees. There was no thought of grand escape, or retribution, or how she should have listened to Fred, there was only the raw and primal urge to survive. Behind her, Gerald ingested the last morsel that was once Fred's brain and let the body drop to the floor. Then he rose and headed out the door to devour the last of his friends.

Heedless of any possible danger the dark woods could offer an unarmed and defenseless woman of her tiny stature, Jan plunged ever deeper, intent only on putting as much distance between her and...and...*it* as possible. Her brain tried to justify what she'd witnessed, but there was nothing logical or otherwise about the scenario. She had to accept that what she saw was... There were lights up ahead! Lights on the road! She welcomed the change of thought and with renewed energy sprinted to her potential salvation. It was a pickup truck! The headlights of a vehicle! There was a man sitting on the hood of the pickup, a large man! Jan knew she was safe without even seeing the face of her new hero.

Gerald lost little time chasing after her. The hunger propelled him after his prey unerringly and his legs felt no strain or exhaustion. Brightness ahead of his quarry signified that there were even more meals beyond the woods and drew him like a moth. He trudged forward at an unfaltering pace, casually closing the distance between him and the release from his pain.

*"Brains..."*

A noise answered Gerald's grumbling.

*Crack!*

Jan saw the muzzle flash and swore she felt the bullet fly past her, but she had no fear...of the bullet anyway. She sprinted faster, stopping only when she had managed to half jump and half climb atop the hood of the pickup truck. She huddled there in a shivering mass of panic behind her newfound guardian.

*Crack!*

The sound echoed again through the surrounding countryside and time seemed to freeze, while the echo slowly faded.

Gerald felt a new sensation—wind blowing directly through his brain cavity. He dropped to his knees as electric pulses no longer provided commands to his limbs. In one short instance and with one cool evening breeze, all of the pain had stopped. Gerald's body fell backwards, bending unnaturally atop itself, and for the first time since his morning swim, he knew peace.

Only when she was sure the thing was no longer chasing her, did Jan look up to see who her rescuer was. Shock and relief washed over her tiny face as Karl looked over at her. Silence washed over the scene as she dove into Karl's arms, feeling more safe and secure than she had felt in years.

"There, there, Janet. It's all right now." Karl put his arm around her and she clung to him like a lifeline.

"I'm sorry we...I was so rude...I..." Jan stammered between sobs.

"Ah know. Ah figured you didn't want me to embarrass you in front of your friends. I can forgive you for being rude, but there's one thing I simply will not abide. Zombies."

Despite her recent trauma, Jan managed a small laugh and hugged Karl even tighter.

"You know, tomorrow's Christmas Eve and ah'm smokin' a turkey. You gonna be home for Christmas this year?" He slowly walked her to the passenger door of the pickup and helped her inside.

"Turkey? You know I'm a veg..." the words trailed off into meaninglessness under Karl's quirked eyebrow. "Turkey sounds great. I'd love to be home for Christmas." She paused and then added, "Dad."

## Epilogue

Karl and Janet set up the tree and decorated it that night, all the while listening to Christmas songs on Karl's favorite radio station. In the morning, Jan awoke in her old bed as the first rays of a brand new day shone through her window. The smells of smoked turkey wafted on the breeze and she knew this would be the best Christmas ever.

Or at least one she would never forget.

# THE FIRST DAYS OF CHRISTMAS

MICAHEL D. GRIFFITHS

## The First Day of Christmas

I've always tried to do what my wife asked of me, especially when it came to taking care of our last remaining child. We once had three, but lost our oldest before the news of the plague had even reached us. Then our middle child died before we could make it clear of the city.

The following weeks had been hard, not just physically, but emotionally. We survived by finding the loneliest canyon in northern Arizona we could. Pariah Canyon didn't have much going for it other than the view and the thin stream of orange-tinged water that passed through its shaded beaches, but it was enough to survive as long as one didn't mind eating fish three times a day.

I always wanted to laugh, and would have if I'd anyone around whose life hadn't become a black pit of complete despair, people that had talked about their zombie survival plans. All that speculation and effort they've given those empty methods of survival, when in the end, all they had to do was reach an isolated area. As long as there was water and food, nothing would bother them. The nearest real town was over a hundred miles away, and since we'd been in our lonely canyon, not so much as a single zombie had braved the series of cliffs required to reach us.

Maybe it wasn't fun, maybe it wasn't even too interesting, but we were safe. As long as we stayed away from the cities and towns, we were safe.

The problem was…that was where my wife wanted me to go.

Not much brought her out of her dark lingering depression. She would keep my son safe when I had to gather firewood and such things, but as the weeks passed, I came to almost feel like she was only a few shades shy of being a zombie herself. She rarely spoke and making love had become a distant memory.

So it was a surprise to me when she asked, or perhaps I should say demanded, that little Lewis have a real Christmas.

When I'd asked what this meant, she'd said, "Well, new toys of course, and a decent meal." She'd gone on to suggest ham, since there could be some left in tins if I looked hard enough. I explained to her that even canned ham needed to be refrigerated, but she was adamant that perhaps there was one kind that didn't need to be. I didn't argue, there was no point. Once my wife had an idea, nothing would change her mind. Still, it was what I loved about her.

As she ran through other items on her fantasy shopping list, I saw a new light in her eyes. This was making her excited, and hopeful. I didn't want to go, but if it would make my wife happy then I really had no choice.

I quickly realized that a trip to Lee's Ferry wouldn't do. I was going to have to visit Page to get the things she wanted. Page was a city of nearly fifty thousand.

One versus fifty thousand.

Great.

Fucking Christmas.


## The Second Day of Christmas

So I headed out with the biggest backpack I owned strapped to my back. It was close to empty, but I certainly didn't look forward to the return trip. Also with me was my two-page shopping list, my six foot spear, and my revolver. We only had two guns; the revolver that had once belonged to my father and the M-16 I'd taken off a dead soldier.

I left the rifle with her, if for no other reason than it would be one less heavy thing for me to lug around.

The forty-three extra bullets I had for my pistol bounced in my front shirt pockets, as I headed down the long trail leading back toward marble canyon.

Fifteen miles is a long way to walk in the desert, and by the time I reached the trail head, I felt beyond exhausted. Deciding to camp at the end of the canyon and start fresh the next day might have been one of my better plans.

Part of me wanted to raid Lee's Ferry for beer, but I figured I'd made it this long without any and didn't want to do anything to endanger my mission before it started.

## The Third Day of Christmas

I'd expected to see a lot of things along the way to Page, but what I saw on the Marble Canyon Bridge I wouldn't have guessed even if I was given twenty tries.

Seven men. Seven living, breathing men, were camped out in the middle of the bridge.

I could see some advantages, such as they could only be assaulted in two directions. Zombies could also be tossed over the side. But it became apparent that this wasn't these men's primary goal.

They controlled the bridge for their own gain, and most likely were living off the tolls they took from any poor survivors traveling in this direction.

If there were any doubts about the quality of their character, the sounds of screaming coming from the woman they were taking turns raping in their RV let me know where they stood.

## The Fourth Day of Christmas

The only thing worse than walking all the way to a town just to find it picked clean, was knowing that it was the only town within thirty miles of where I was camping. Having seven raping mad men downstream from where my wife camped didn't raise my spirits much either.

I guess the only upside was that those guys had cleaned the town of Lee's Ferry of zombies, too. They'd left a few things in the store, but the hot diet soda didn't really hit the spot. I was still going to Page, but I had to check this town out first, just in case I'd been wrong, which I wasn't.

A sigh escaped from me as my thoughts of cleverly luring a few dozen zombies at the marauders faded. I was the only guy in a world full of zombies that couldn't even find one.

As if mocking my thoughts, a lone zombie moaned in the distance.

I stood up. My eyes strained, but yeah, it was just one. On a lark I started to walk back toward the bridge. Of course it followed me. I led it off-road, so maybe the guys on the bridge wouldn't spot us as easily, even if I had no clue what I was trying to do.

Then I spotted something.

As I moved past one of the Grand Canyon River rafting companies, I spotted a small, inflatable emergency boat in the window. One rock through the window later, I had my hands on the small bundle, which was only a little larger than a car battery.

I flipped the zombie the bird and began to jog north by northeast.

Climbing down the almost sheer cliff of Marble Canyon wasn't the easiest thing I'd ever did, but I made it. I would have climbed three times the length in order to avoid having to navigate the small boat across the mighty Colorado.

Water splashed and I had of course forgotten to grab a paddle. Every inch of me became soaked before I'd been on the river for thirty seconds. I paddled as hard as I could with my hands as a wall of white water rose to meet me. My white-knuckled fingers clutched the sides of the inflatable boat as I somehow hung on.

But I had a new problem. It was taking me so long to cross the river that my neon-yellow boat was about to reach the bridge. I hung on tight as I neared the bridge. I expected shouts and maybe a bullet to the brain any moment, but nothing of the sort happened, and I floated under the bridge and flew past it safely.

Well, safely might have been an exaggeration.

I swallowed more water than my canteen held, but I was able to reach an area where the eastern bank calmed. A minute later, my exhausted form slumped down on the shore. Again I was miles away from anything resembling a zombie. I joked with myself about being the most zombie-free man on Earth, while I set up the boat like a half-assed tent.

Shade had already claimed the canyon and soon exhaustion claimed me.

## The Fifth Day of Christmas

I awoke to something touching me.

I started thrashing and kicking. I grabbed at something and it felt slimy and wet. Round-gray eyes met mine over a pale swollen body.

Bile rose in my mouth as I realized I had a bloated drowning victim assaulting me. The only thing that had kept me alive was the river fish, the same fish that had eaten away at the thing's fingers and toes to the point where I doubted it could walk.

I aimed a kick at it and flinched when my boot smashed half its face away from its skull. I almost shot it, but thought better; I remained too close to the bridge. So, after scrambling to my feet, I put the nasty thing out of its misery with a large river rock.

After catching my breath, I checked to make sure there weren't any more.

I felt pretty good about things until I noticed that one of the splintered bones at the end of the zombie's fingers had slashed a wide hole in the raft.

It looked like I would need to find another way over the river on the way back.

I ate some dried fish, then looked for an easy route up the eastern side of Marble Canyon. There was no such thing as an easy route up the side of Marble Canyon, but I found a place that wouldn't automatically be my doom, and huffed and puffed my way through the morning.

I was about halfway up when I heard gunshots coming from the bridge. There were only a few at first, but then they became a constant.

It sounded like those a-holes were getting into some serious trouble. Served them right.

With a renewed feeling that there might be some level of justice lingering in the world, I finished climbing and didn't stop walking until I'd reached the bottom of the mountain range surrounding Page.


## The Sixth Day of Christmas

It was easy to forget what a difference a car made until I didn't have one. What would have taken me thirty minutes to ascend, took me all day, for I didn't dare use the real road.

Again, the only upside of the long, dangerous, and oh so sweaty climb was that it stayed in zombie-free territory, and there remained no chance in a million years that a zombie could make it within a thousand yards of me without being seen. If I had enough food and water and maybe something to keep me from going crazy, I could have rode out the apocalypse up on those cliffs.

But I would still have needed some serious shade, too.

## The Seventh Day of Christmas

This turned out to be another long day—thirty miles over rough terrain.

I actually encountered a few undead. Some I avoided, but I put down more than my fair share. Again, I had to wonder why more people weren't living up here around the cliffs. I doubted there was a much easier place to put down the damn things.

They see prey and start to stumble towards it, but between the uneven ground and the rigid cliffs, the dead tend to topple and usually break an ankle or leg. Once I get to them after that, it's pretty easy to pin them down with my spear and chop their heads off with a few whacks of an axe.

I have mixed feelings about killing zombies. My initial thought was that it's so gross that it could be the type of thing that could change a man, leave him jaded. Case in point—the rogues on the bridge. I doubted most of them would have been raping some poor girl two months ago, but look at them now.

Even though I'd like to see them all permanently dead, and would like to pitch in killing them, too, I also tended to feel that the percentages were against me as far as a long term survival rate went. Sure, a healthy person could kill a zombie or two if they were careful, but all it took was one mistake, one tooth scraping my hand, and then I was done for.

Say a person was ninety-nine percent perfect with his kills, that still meant that if he killed a hundred zombies, something could go wrong—and something could always go wrong. In fact, when a person was alone with no one to watch their back, something could definitely go wrong.

At one point during the walk, I had two undead on my tail. So I pushed the first one into a dry wash, and while trying to push the second one over a cliff, my foot got jammed between two rocks. I managed to get it out okay without any damage, but with a broken ankle out here, it would have been just as bad as a zombie bite. If that had happened, I'm not sure if I'd even have bothered to try and make it back to my wife through all the canyons and the heat.

Looking down at my pistol, I shivered at the thought of having to use it on myself

By the end of the day, I could see Page from the rise I'd climbed to the top of. Even from the distance, I could see the dead moving around on the streets. No signs of true life or resistance were evident.

I'd made it, but exhaustion owned me, so I climbed up to the top of a peak and got myself a good night sleep, before heading into that Hell hole.

* * *

Time was like a twisted weight on my shoulders. My wife wanted me back by Christmas and I'd already used over half the days I had and I still hadn't even gotten one thing on her damn list.

I checked my pistol and grabbed up my spear and set off to the town that quite possibly would be my doom.

As I neared, I came across a vehicle parked in the middle of the road. Its passenger door was open. I approached slowly. The insides were such a mess that, even after all I'd been through, it was a struggle to keep down my meager breakfast.

A corpse that would never be whole enough to reanimate sat, still buckled, in the driver's seat. The rest of the interior was awash with blood that had long since turned black. Yet, despite this horror, something caught my attention—the key in the ignition.

Pushing back my disgust, I turned the key. The battery worked, but the empty light on the gas gauge came on.

Moving to the other side of the car, I opened the driver's door, and with a quick and quite revolting jerk, I pulled the body free of the car.

After popping the trunk, I found a small plastic jerry can. It would have to do. After searching my area, I noticed another parked car in the distance. I began to jog toward it. Bad idea, though, as my jogging attracted the damn zombies nearby. I made it to the vehicle okay, but had no way to siphon out the gas—if there was any in it to begin with. So, after drawing my knife, I located the gas tank and stabbed into it, again and again. All the while the moaning of the zombies grew louder in my ears.

I had just poked a hole through the gas tank and placed the jerry can under a small leak when something grabbed my shoulders. Without thinking, I turned and stabbed the thing. The good news was the knife stuck the zombie deep in the temple, the bad news, though, was its limp form pulled the knife from my hands as it slumped to the ground.

More bad news; seven other zombies were closing in on me. I took down one with a spear through the face, but the weapon quickly became too awkward to use as they moved in. Against my better judgment, I drew my pistol and fired point blank into the closest three. This allowed me to run past them. Once past, them I lured them away from the car and prepared myself to fight. I wasn't leaving, I need that damn gas.

More coming in every direction, attracted to the activity, but they came in twos and threes, and though it was difficult, eventually I managed to take them all down. Still, it wasn't something I would want to do again. I was lucky, damn lucky, that I hadn't been bit or scratched.

After some more maneuvering, I managed to kill each of them with my spear.

I only had a half gallon or so of fuel, but it would have to be enough, because when I looked up after fueling up the first car with my purloined gas, I saw what could only be called a horde coming my way from every direction. After upending the gas into the tank to get as much as possible, I hurried into the blood-soaked driver's seat just as the first group of undead arrived. Their gruesome hands were already slapping against the windows before I had even tried the ignition. "This had better work, or this'll be all she wrote."

More zombies joined their bloody fellows.

I turned the key and said a silent prayer. The engine resisted for a moment, but then turned over. I hadn't been so happy since I'd lost my virginity.

A yell of delight escaped my lips and I hurried to drive forward before the zombies grew too thick. A minute later, I was weaving through the growing crowd of undead, heading toward my destiny or my doom.

## The Eighth Day of Christmas

Even though the undead remained thick, I slowed down before reaching Page. I pulled out my wife's Christmas wish list and reviewed it one more time. It seemed like I'd have to hit a shopping mall to meet her demands, and I wondered if Page even had one.

"I guess it's time to find out," I mumbled as I drove on.

Driving through Page was like bouncing through a pinball machine full of teeth. Cars all but blocked the roads and zombies leapt out at me every ten seconds. I had almost given up hope and figured that I'd be forced to piecemeal my looting from different stores, when I spotted the mall on the top of a hill behind the city hall building.

I floored it.

As I drew near, it surprised me to find that the security grates hadn't been dropped over the outer doorways to the building. "Screw it," I said aloud and drove straight through the front entrance of Sears.

There were zombies inside, but not too many. I only saw four or five before my car went through the clothing racks and sped into the mall's interior.

Checking my list again, I mentally figured out where and what to do next. I could only carry so much back to Pariah Canyon, but this hadn't shortened my wife's list which began with some of the items she wanted for herself.

After pausing for a moment to load my gun, I drove the car to the women's department, the front bumper shoving racks of clothing out of the way the entire time. I ran over two female zombies, that I swore looked like they were shopping, and then the car skidded to a stop on the polished tile.

I quickly grabbed armfuls of clothes and other items my wife wanted. I could sort through them later or come back to get multiple loads from the car if needed. I was almost done before the first zombies showed up. I took careful aim and killed the closest three with the gun, then hurried back to the car.

Next was the cooking department, which luckily was on the same floor as the clothing. My wife had asked for a cast iron pan, so I grabbed four of then for the hell of it. A few pots and utensils and even spices went in next. I even found some cans of SPAM on the back of a bottom shelf. It wasn't ham, but then the SPAM didn't need to be refrigerated either. It was close enough to what my wife had asked for.

I paused to shoot a few more zombies, and then ran out of rounds. "Forget it," I said and just jumped back into the car before the dead grew too thick around me. Once more shoving racks of clothing out of the way, I began driving.

I considered getting some things for myself, but the gun racks had been raided and I knew I had more than I could carry as it was, so I just blew off my needs. I was driving through the store when I saw the boots in the footwear section.

New boots wouldn't be something I would have to carry…

I couldn't help myself, and I stopped the car and got out, the engine idling softly.

Not having time to check sizes, I just grabbed an armful and tossed them into the back seat. I was about to leave, when the men's department caught my eye, and the section where men's pants were clearly visible. I knew I shouldn't, but I couldn't help myself, and I ran over there. I grabbed an armful of jeans about my size then ran back toward the car. The zombies were getting thicker as they followed the wide path of destruction the car had made through the store, and a sinking feeling overwhelmed me when I remembered that I hadn't reloaded the gun.

I looked around for a weapon I could use, but could only see clothing. Turning sideways, I kicked the closest zombie into a circular rack of t-shirts; it went tumbling over.

Then I saw a rectangular clothes bin in front of me. It was on wheels. Without thinking it through, I grabbed it, dropped my armful of jeans into the bin, and began using it like a battering ram to try to clear away the bodies before me. It worked, but three more still lunged towards me from both my left and right. I pushed the bin to the right, which slowed down the walking corpses on that side, but one of the zombies to the left was only a few feet away.

Not knowing what else to do, I tossed a pair of jeans at its face. It growled, but then tripped over the jeans as they fell to the floor. As the zombie went down, it tripped up another one that had been right behind it. Now there remained just one zombie between me and the car. I grabbed a pair of jeans from the bin and rushed by the fallen zombies, then ducked under another zombie's flailing arms, before dashing back to the car. More zombies converged from every side, but I'd made it to the opened driver's door with my prize in hand.

I might have been yelling my own praises and singing one of my favorite songs, when I remembered my son. I still had to stop off at the toy store to get him some things, otherwise the entire trip would have been for nothing—or mostly nothing.

Driving through the mall had increased in difficulty now; all the undead had realized that something was going on and had come out to see. I tried to avoid as many of them as I could, but if one smashed out its unlife on my bumper, I didn't bust out crying.

I drove by the toy store first to check it out. Most of the toys were in the back of the store that would be age appropriate for my son. It was tempting to just drive into the store, but there might be a chance I could get stuck in there and I would still have to get out of the car anyway.

Then I passed by a service entrance. Its double doors would be just wide enough to get the car through.

Back when I was in college, I'd worked for a furniture store in a mall and had learned that most of the malls had hallways running behind the stores, which were used for deliveries. Trusting that this mall was the same, I drove to the double doors.

Now, someone else might have just crashed through them, but I wanted to keep my trail clear, so grabbing two of the frying pans, I stopped just shy of the doors. No zombies had reached me yet, so I rushed to the doors and flung them open.

It was a bad idea.

Three zombies had been lingering on the other side, perhaps too stupid to figure out how to escape from the hallway.

I yelped loudly, while quickly backpedaling until my butt hit the gore-splattered front of my car. As they reached for me, the frying pan in my right hand flew out and hit one of them in the side of the head so hard that it dropped to the floor instantly. More surprised than relieved, I pummeled the others with every ounce of strength I had. Soon, my world became a whirlwind of ringing metal and rancid blood. I managed to lay out the other two zombies without getting hurt myself, but I knew my luck was running out.

I had new problems, too.

The entire mall of undead had flooded into the hallway leading to the double doors. There was no way to get back into the car without being torn apart.

Not knowing what else to do, I ran.

The toy store was to the right of me, so I ran in that direction. As the undead poured into the back hallway, I finally remembered my pistol jammed into my belt. I threw the frying pans into the faces of the leading zombies and then ran to the door that led to the back of the toy store. Some luck remained with me, for at least the doors were labeled and I knew I was going in the right direction.

My trembling hands hurried to load the gun. With the horde coming up behind me, I opened the back door to the toy store as quietly as I could.

I didn't see a thing to oppose me. Not one zombie barred my way or sought my flesh. I went into the store and felt relieved when I was able to lock the door behind me.

I thought that maybe I had a chance after all. That I could get through this intact with a few presents for my family.

That was when they saw me and I reconsidered everything.

They must have started Christmas early in Page, because there was a Santa, but not like one I had ever seen. The red of his garb had become the most gore splattered thing I'd ever seen. The blood had long since turned black, but this wasn't what caught my eye and had my heart stuck in my throat. Interwoven through the Santa zombie's white beard were the remains of his past feasts, which included several fingers that had once belonged to children.

Surrounding him on the floor were his moaning victims. Never had I seen people more eaten and yet still reanimated as zombies—and they were all children!

Like a pool of moving viscera the devoured children flopped and quivered. In some cases the bodies were little more than heads clinging to threads of gore. Other bodies struggle to roll toward me, but lacked the arms and legs to do so. Blackened bones and stiff organs littered the floor until it became difficult to tell where one child ended and the other began.

Despite the danger of the colossal undead Santa lurching towards me, I emptied the contents of my stomach across the floor. This gave the giant Santa enough time to reach me. I brought up my gun, but it was slapped out of my hands to go sliding across the bloody tiles. I tried to move, but my foot landed on a kidney. Losing my balance, I fell to the floor.

I struggled through the violent mess, as the mouths of small children snapped at me from every side.

Santa grabbed a fistful of my hair and leaned in for a bite.

I fumbled for anything I could use to defend myself, as the small teeth snapped and fought to land a bite. Then my hands landed on something, but only when after I'd jammed it into Santa's rotten mouth, did I realize that it was one of those yellow preschool-colored ring stackers.

This bought me enough time to break away, as the demon of Christmas needed to use both hands to pull the toy free. Moving on my hands and knees, I made it to an aisle and hurried down it. Somehow, through all the chaos, I realized that this would also be the right aisle to find toys for my son.

Then the giant Santa came lumbering after me. It growled while thrashing through the racks of toys behind me. Searching for a weapon, my eyes landed on a big metal fire truck.

It would have to do.

Struggling to my feet, I lifted the truck and smashed the son of a bitch in the side of the face, but the zombie still came at me like a runway bulldozer. I smashed it again and again while its clawing fingers tried to get a grip on me. Then its fingers found a hold on my shirt and pulled me in for a life-ending bite.

That was when I raised my arms, the toy truck still clutched in my hands. I would only have time for one more blow, so I put everything I had into slamming the truck down on the center of Santa's head.

The truck broke apart on impact, but so did undead St. Nick's skull.

As the red-garbed body slumped to the floor, I stood there just trying to breathe. It was the sounds of the zombies banging on the door to the hallway that pulled me back to the dangers I still faced.

After cleaning myself up, I located my gun where it had fallen and looked out into the mall. It appeared to be almost empty. I wondered why until I realized that most of the zombies must have followed me into the service hallway.

Moving as quietly as I could, I gathered some toys for my son and made my way past the devoured children to the front of the store. Again, the zombies appeared to be few and far between, so I hurried to the car.

I suffered through a few minutes of worry when I saw that several zombies were lingering around the vehicle. Still, with the motor running, it helped conceal the noise of my movement and I dashed to the car, getting in before most of them even knew I was there. Then it became a simple matter to backtrack my way out of the mall and back onto the main road.

Dodging zombies as needed, I just drove for a few minutes, trying to piece together what my next move should be.

I'd completed part of my mission, but it wouldn't mean shit if I couldn't get what I'd gathered back to my wife and son. My thoughts went to Marble Canyon and the blocked bridge. How could I cross it without being shot, the car taken from me and no doubt the toys and other supplies I'd collected?

Then they car reached a rise and the giant form of Lake Powell opened up before me. I smiled to myself and figured I'd found a way to get across after all. I'd take a boat.

And finding the boat itself turned out to be surprisingly easy. There were still a few rental boats fueled and ready. Most of what had once been there was missing, and I worried that any survivors living on the lake might find me, but I was willing to take the chance. Besides, I figured most of them would be hiding in the canyons and not traveling in the open near the dam.

A few zombies lingered around the dock, but a few well-placed shots got me and my presents into a big house boat. At first the engine didn't want to turn over, and as more zombies appeared on the dock, I feared I wouldn't be able to make it to a different boat before being overwhelmed. But on the seventh try the motor fired up, and a minute later I was cruising across the lake and mooring on the far side, where on the Utah side of the lake there was a small beach parking lot littered with cars, but only had a few zombies. After killing the undead, it took a while to find a car that still had its keys and would start. But I found one where the owner must have been in such a hurry that he'd not only left the car door open, but the keys were still in the ignition.

Luckily it turned over on the third try, too. I drove it back to the house boat, loaded up the presents, and as the first few of a new group of zombies began to come closer, I drove off in a cloud of orange dust and sand.

## The Ninth Day of Christmas

It was sad to leave the car behind, but it was useless once it ran out of gas. The hike to Pariah Canyon from the north was difficult under the best of circumstances, but when I was running low on food and carrying about seventy pounds of presents, I was far from being anywhere near the best of circumstances.

At least I had gone a whole day without seeing a single zombie.

One must always enjoy the small things in life.

## The Tenth Day of Christmas

I cursed the heat.

I cursed my load.

I cursed the walking dead.

I cursed my wife for making me leave the safety of the camp on a fool's errand.

But in the end I mostly just cursed myself as my legs slowly ate up the dusty, rock-covered miles.

## The Eleventh Day of Christmas: Christmas Eve

I realized it was Christmas Eve.

How was my family doing? Was my wife able to catch enough fish for them? Would my son be okay without me there? What if the dead had found their way into the canyon? I knew I couldn't afford to think about it. I just had to keep going.

As I drew closer, my family's fate lay heavier on my mind than my own. They'd been over ten days without my help and protection. Were they still okay?

And, I know it sounded stupid, but I really wanted to be there on Christmas. All the effort would have been for nothing if I couldn't have a real Christmas with my family. I tried and tried to make it to them by Christmas Eve, but as darkness set it, getting lost became a concern and I had to give up for the night.

## Christmas Day

Two miles out from my camp, I noticed the tracks. At first I thought zombies, but they were too regular, too even. The body came next. One of their own. I looked closer. Despite the bite on his arm, the guy had never become a zombie.

I'm no tracker, but I was pretty sure there were only two of them and the tracks seemed recent. Thoughts of men doing to my wife what I heard those bastards doing to that poor girl…on…the…bridge.

Then it occurred to me. Those men had been overrun. Maybe a few of them had escaped. Who else would be around?

I quickened my pace. Rapists were heading toward my wife and on fucking Christmas day.

* * *

I wanted to sneak up on the camp from behind, but that would have me going through thick clusters of half-dead trees. Staying silent would be nearly impossible, too. The other option would be quieter, but using the main trail along the river would expose me to anyone for a hundred yards.

Even from where I was crouched behind the last bend, I heard the men laughing.

"Looks like we got ourselves a Christmas present this year after all."

"No doubt. But what should we do with the kid, Burt?"

"I'm not sure. We could maybe eat him I suppose."

This brought out a muffled cry from my wife and I figured one of them had a hand clamped over her mouth. I had to think quickly; they might be about to kill my son.

Then I had an idea; it was probably a stupid idea, but I never claimed to be a genius. I'm just a man that was smart enough to know that sticking to the wilderness meant I'd be getting the least amount of trouble from the zombies and men like these. If I could just get rid of them, it might be the best Christmas present I could ever give my family.

I heard my son crying as I lowered my heavy pack to the ground. I checked to make sure my gun and knife were secure before leaning my spear against the canyon wall. I hated to leave it behind, but my plan wouldn't work with me carrying it.

"Shut that kid up," Burt snapped. "I want to be able to enjoy this."

I had no idea how the guy intended to shut up my son, but figured it would be better if I never found out. So I lunged forward into the tangled woods behind the camp. I clung as close to the cliff face as I could while releasing my best impression of a hungry zombie's moan.

It got their attention.

"Shit, one of those things must have followed us here."

"It sounds like there's only one," Burt said. "Go take it out, Eddy. But don't use your gun if you can avoid it. We don't want any others to figure out where we are. We wouldn't want anything to destroy our Christmas. Right, little lady?"

I could see my wife struggling with the man, while my son grabbed her leg and tried to pull her away from the bastard.

He'd always been a good boy.

Eddy picked up an axe by the fire pit and came walking towards me. I tried to keep the zombie act up. My stiff legs moved in awkward jerks while my moans echoed through the canyon.

Eddy raised the axe as he drew closer.

I turned towards him and hurried as much as I dared. I needed to be as close to my family as I could before I changed tactics.

"Come here, you dirty son of a bitch," Eddy swore. "You bastards killed a lot of good men on the bridge."

"That's not how I see it!" I yelled, as I drew the gun and shot the man in the face. He didn't even have time to scream before his head jerked back and he hit the ground hard.

"What the hell!" Burt yelled and tried to draw his pistol, but my wife grabbed one of the fingers on the hand he had over her mouth, and twisted it back so far that it must have broken. He yelled again, but in pain this time.

My wife got loose, but he still had his pistol out. "One more move and I'll blow the kid away!" he shouted. But in his haste he hadn't pointed the gun in my son's direction.

I ran straight at him, firing as I ran.

I'm not the best shot. The first few rounds went wide, and it gave Burt enough time to return fire. I figured I'd feel the agony of a bullet ripping through me at any moment.

But then, on my fourth shot, the bullet hit him in the shoulder and he spun back around. I dropped to one knee and aimed again. My last bullet took him dead center in the middle of the chest. He fell back, this time down for good.

My wife rushed into my arms while my son shouted, "Daddy!" over and over.

"I love you. I knew you'd save us," she cried in relief.

"I love you too, honey, but I think we should make sure that bastard's gun is secure.

She rushed from my arms like she'd been hugging a rattlesnake, knowing I was right.

I moved over to Burt and picked up his fallen pistol. He didn't look too good. He appeared to be having trouble breathing and pink bubbles appeared on his lips. "You can't kill me," he breathed.

"I think I already did."

"But there are so few of us left."

I raised the pistol and aimed between his eyes. "All the more reason to make sure only the good ones make it."

I squeezed the trigger.

* * *

I probably shouldn't end the story without letting you know that my son loved all the new toys I'd brought him. He kept repeating "Daddy" while he played and I got a hug about every five minutes.

My wife looked very pleased with her gifts as well. The spices brought forth a series of kisses that left me gasping for air.

In the end, due to our last series of circumstances, I had a Christmas as well. For the men from the bridge were loaded with gear, firearms, and even a fair amount of food. We splurged that night and made a regular feast, which centered around the SPAM I'd found. In most ways, I'd have to say it was the best Christmas I'd ever had.

# 12/25

DANIEL LOUBIER

"Jake!" Tom yelled from the other end of the house. "Hand me the gun, quick!"

Jake jumped to his feet, ran through the living room and toward the hall.

"I can't reach it," Tom said. His voice was strained, as if his current position prevented him from being able to speak easily.

Jake reached the hall and looked to the end, where Tom was sitting on the floor, squeezed awkwardly in an open doorway.

A DeWalt nail gun lay just out of Tom's reach. "I've got the new frame shimmed perfectly, but I have to nail a piece of sheetrock back in place."

Jake walked the rest of the way, leaned down to pick up the nail gun, and handed it to Tom.

"Sit right here real quick," Tom added. He took the DeWalt with one hand and patted the door jamb with the other. "Just put some pressure here. This won't take long."

"Okay," Jake said.

It was Christmas Day. Their parents, both retired, had decided to spend the holidays in the Caribbean that year. As a surprise gift, Tom and Jake were replacing all the interior doors of their parents' 1950s-style Cape. Their mother had always adored the 'cottage' look of so many of the homes in their area, so her two sons had purchased all new doors, which Tom had been able to find at a considerable discount. Their plan was to replace the old doors with the new ones before their parents returned from vacation.

Jake pressed his weight against the new door jamb while Tom squeezed off a few nails. *Thunk! Thunk! Thunk!*

"Okay," Tom said. "Step out and let me back in there."

Jake stood to the side while Tom returned to the door jamb. With trained precision he eyed the space where the new pieces of trim would sit along the new jamb. A builder for over two decades, Tom was never satisfied with *good enough*. It had to be perfect. And if it wasn't perfect…he would *make* it perfect.

"Looks pretty good, little brother! Huh?"

Jake, hardly a 'little brother' at thirty-two years old, nodded. "Looks awesome."

"Yeah," Tom said. "I still can't believe what we paid for them. Dad's gonna think we spent a fortune!" He laughed.

"That's the idea, right?"

"You got it!" His eyes lightened. Tom had spent Christmas morning with his wife and two children. Since their parents were out of town, Tom had invited Jake to open presents with the kids, which Jake had happily accepted. Jake was recently single, and fresh off a recent break with his longtime girlfriend, and the time spent with his niece and nephew had been the perfect remedy for the break-up blues. Afterward, Tom's wife, Liz, had taken the kids to her parents' house for more presents and, later, dinner.

Tom and Jake had been hard at work all afternoon. They had installed all the bedroom doors and two closets. All that remained was the bathroom door.

"What time are you guys having dinner?" Jake asked.

"Five-thirty."

Jake nodded. "What time is it now?"

Tom looked at his watch. "Three o'clock on the nose. Plenty of time to get the bathroom door in."

"Cool."

"Be right back." Tom slipped past Jake and disappeared down the hallway. The last new door was outside, lying in the bed of Tom's pickup truck.

While Jake waited for Tom to return, he stood and admired his older brother's work. Perfect lines, impeccable workmanship. He opened and closed the door several times. Each time the door latched smoothly and effortlessly. He opened it halfway…it did not sway in either direction. Perfect balance. A muffled *crack* sounded and he wondered if something was suddenly amiss with one of the hinges.

"Jake!"

Though all the windows were closed in the house, Jake distinctly heard his brother's voice from outside.

"Jake, get out here!" Tom yelled before Jake could even muster a response.

Jake hurried to the front of the house, half-expecting to see Tom laboring under the weight of a brand new door, but he found his brother squatting low to the ground next to the pickup. Jake pushed open the front door. "What's…"

"Get over here!" Tom hissed.

Jake scurried to Tom's side, ducking his head along the way, but not quite understanding why.

"What is it?" Jake whispered.

"I think I just heard someone scream."

Jake squeezed his eyebrows together. "Like…*serious* scream, or playing around?"

Tom looked at him dubiously. "Really? What do you think?"

"*Help!*"

Jake's head went up. He glanced at Tom, who only nodded, his eyes wide. The cry for help had come from behind their parents' house. A small cul-de-sac neighborhood bordered the property in the back. The scream had certainly come from one of the houses back there. Jake's eyes followed the driveway to their parents' detached garage. The space between the house and the garage created a narrow line of sight to the backyard. He could just see the side of the neighbor's yard.

*"Help!"*

"Let's go," Tom said. "Follow me."

Jake followed his brother along the side of his pickup and up the driveway. Tom then stayed close to the garage while offering hand signals for his brother to follow.

*"Somebody help, please!"*

"Jesus Christ, Tom…"

"Shhh!"

They reached the back corner of the garage and squatted again. The last call for help had been much louder than before—the activity was certainly happening in the house directly behind their parents' home.

Tom pulled out his cell phone.

"You calling the police?" Jake asked.

"Hell yeah."

As Tom started to dial out, a door opened at the neighbor's house. He and Jake stared. A man wearing a white t-shirt and patterned flannel pants stumbled out the door. He almost fell as he staggered along the front porch and down the steps. From their disadvantaged angle, they could both see the man was clutching his neck. He appeared to be running away, but from what, they couldn't immediately tell. After the man cleared the steps and made it to the front yard, Tom and Jake could see what impaired him.

Blood gushed and sprayed over the man's fingers and knuckles and onto his shirt, leaving a large red mess that grew with each labored step. He had clearly suffered a devastating neck injury. His voice was garbled as he continued to call out for help.

"Oh my God," Tom gasped in horror. "Hey, Mister…" he started to call out, but someone else emerged from the house.

A man wearing a Santa Claus outfit crashed through the door and stumbled onto the lawn.

"What the fu…" Jake began. Then he grabbed Tom's arm. "Did you call the cops yet?"

"Shit, no." Tom dialed the phone quickly and they both continued to watch the scene unfold barely a hundred feet away.

"I don't believe this," Jake said. "Should we help him? We should, right?"

"Wait, let me—hello?" Tom said into the phone. "Hi, my name's Tom Vernon. I'm at my parents' house at three-four-zero Candywood Ave. Someone's hurt. It looks like a neighbor was just assaulted by another man."

In the background, the injured neighbor continued to call out for help as the man dressed as Santa slowly chased after him.

Jake studied the second man closely. Dressed as Santa, he wore what looked like a red mask over his beard. It seemed rather large and unusual; it was another moment until Jake realized it wasn't a mask.

*Oh my God…* he thought.

Santa's mouth and beard was caked in blood. Whose blood was the big question, and Jake feared it belonged to the neighbor.

"Yes," Tom continued into his phone. "We're in the backyard." There was a brief pause. "My brother and I." Another pause, then, "They both left the house. The one man is calling for help. There's a lot of blood. Should we…no? A weapon? I can't tell…" He turned quickly to Jake. "Can you tell if the guy is holding a weapon?"

Jake shook his head.

"No," Tom said into the phone. "We don't see a weapon but I can't say for sure if he has one or not."

"What are they saying?" Jake whispered.

Tom held up a hand. The neighbor, having crossed into another neighbor's yard, had disappeared from view, but Jake could still hear him desperately calling out for help.

Santa continued to follow after him.

"Okay," Tom said into the phone. "We'll just wait until—right."

A moment later, distant sirens could be heard.

"Yes," Tom said. "We can hear them. Please hurry. Okay, thanks. Bye."

"What did they say?" Jake asked.

"They said I'm the third person to call in about this in the past minute or so. They said to sit tight but don't interfere. So far, no one else who's called can say for sure if the other guy has a weapon, and the cops don't want anyone else getting hurt."

"What the hell, man."

"I know," Tom said. "This is so fucked up. You saw the blood on the guy, right?"

Jake nodded. His face wore a mask of shock.

"Sorry you had to see that, buddy."

Jake found it an odd thing for Tom to say. It wasn't Tom's fault that Jake had seen what he had. Tom shouldn't apologize for anything. Then again, maybe Tom felt responsible for calling Jake outside in the first place. Perhaps Tom, in that moment, thought he should have let Jake stay inside, and he could have dealt with the situation himself.

*Always the big brother*, Jake thought.

The sirens were louder, closer, and Jake surmised they were only a couple blocks away now. They had responded fast, likely because it was the only disturbance in town right now. It was then that an awful realization filled Jake's head; it quickly reached down his spine and settled in his stomach, and knotted everything inside.

"Tom."

"What?"

"I haven't heard that guy call for help lately."

The look in Tom's eyes indicated he hadn't noticed either until that very moment. He stayed quiet and held his breath. Jake did the same. Together, they listened to the immense silence that had replaced the sound of screams. Jake was right, it had been a couple of minutes since they had heard anything from the neighbor. They stared at each other quietly, hoping to hear the injured man call out again, to indicate he was still alive, still breathing.

The sirens were now moving onto the street. Tom looked at Jake and nodded in the direction of the cul-de-sac. It was a subtle question about whether or not he wanted to go check on the neighbor. Jake silently agreed and they both stood. Tom led them through their parents' backyard, into the neighbors' yard, and onto the street. They stopped at what Tom deemed a safe distance from the activity. What they saw froze the blood in Jake's veins.

The neighbor had finally succumbed to his injuries. He was laying on someone's front lawn a few houses down; a blood-drip trail on the asphalt and grass followed him to his final resting place. But seeing the dead body wasn't the worst part.

The man in the Santa outfit was kneeling over the body closely. Neither Tom nor Jake could see what he was doing until an officer jumped out of a squad car and shouted, "Police! Get away from the body! Let me see your hands!"

When Santa looked up, Jake could see what he had been doing. Entrails spilled out of St. Nick's mouth and fell in chunks from his blood-soaked beard. He'd been eating the victim's insides.

Jake curled forward and vomited, then he rested his hands on his knees and heaved again. Tom placed a calm hand on his back and Jake finally dropped down to one knee.

"It's okay, buddy," Tom said. "It's over."

Just then the officer shouted, "Get down, now!"

Jake looked up. Santa was on his feet and walking toward the cop. There was something strange about his gait. He stumbled awkwardly toward the officer, like he was drunk, and Jake wondered how alcohol could have affected somebody in such a maniacal way.

"Get down!" the officer shouted again. He had drawn his gun and was aiming it at Santa, but Santa continued to shamble toward him. Another squad car skidded to a stop and two more officers jumped out.

"Get on the ground!" one of the new officers shouted, and there was a beat before Jake realized the new cop was shouting in his and Tom's direction.

Another beat passed before a second attacker was on Tom.

The attacker lunged, sending Tom forward and into his brother. Jake fell on his side and groaned as the weight of the two bodies punished his frame. He twisted his head to see who or what had delivered the blow. A bloodied face was attached to the back of Tom's neck, and feral growls came from a mouth that was a mess of viscous, pulpy gore.

Tom screamed.

Jake panicked and tried to wiggle free from Tom and his attacker. He could hear shouts all around him, but in his frantic state he couldn't determine what was being said. He fought against the weight of the two people on top of him, but couldn't free himself to be of any help to Tom.

Then a gunshot filled the air! An instant later, a mixture of blood, hair and brain matter sprayed Jake's face. Tom stared at him, his face pale and weak. Jake saw a river of blood pump out of Tom's neck wound in quick, pulsing currents.

"Jake…" Tom struggled to speak. "Ja…"

"Tom," Jake started to say, but he couldn't find the words.

Shadows fell over them and many hands moved the dead body off of Tom. A few more hands pulled Tom away from Jake and laid him on his back. Jake sat up quickly and watched as two paramedics tended fervently to his brother. Then he caught some movement in his periphery and looked around.

In all the chaos, he had not noticed the dozen other squad cars and multiple ambulances that had arrived. The neighborhood had become a multiple crime scene. Teams of uniformed and plain-clothes law enforcement men and women were walking the area. The sound of a helicopter hung in the distance; no doubt a local news affiliate approaching the area to cover the story. Jake had completely forgotten about Santa. He looked around, trying to find him. Then he spotted him. In the street, where Santa had been on his feet only moments ago when he had approached the first responding officer, he was now laying face-down in a motionless pile of soiled red-and-white.

Jake felt a hand on his shoulder and turned to see a bloodied latex glove. His eyes moved up the arm until he stared into a pair of kind, somber blue eyes. The woman's lips moved but Jake didn't hear anything. "What?" he asked.

She said, "Did you know this man?" She gestured to Tom, who was prone on the ground.

"Yes," Jake replied. And after a brief pause added, "He's my brother."

The paramedic's eyes seemed to fall at the sides. "I'm very sorry."

"Wait…what?" Jake was confused. What was happening?

"What was his name?" she continued.

"What do you mean? And why are you talking about him like he's…"

*No.* His heart filled with a burning dread and a desperate plea to erase the paramedic's words raced through the front of his mind.

*No, no, no!*

"I'm so sorry," she said.

Jake grabbed her arm. "Wait!" he begged. His eyes darted back and forth from Tom's unmoving body to the paramedic. "He can't…you have to…just wait!" He was screaming now.

"I'm so sorry, sir," she said again.

Jake felt another pair of hands grab his left arm and shoulder.

"Sir," a male voice said from behind. "I need you to come with me."

Jake swiveled his head to see a uniformed cop. "Huh?"

Nothing was making sense. He and Tom had only come outside to see what the disturbance was. Tom wasn't dead. Was he? No, he couldn't be. He was just there a minute ago, reassuring Jake that everything was going to be okay, and now nothing was okay.

"No," Jake said with confused anger. He tried to pull away from the officer. "My brother isn't…" When he turned back, the paramedics were already moving Tom onto a stretcher and rolling it away. One of them pulled a sheet over Tom's body.

"*No!*" Jake yelled. "He's not dead!"

"Sir," the officer said again, "you need to come with me."

Jake was now struggling against the officer's grip.

"Now is probably not a good time, Brett," the female paramedic said. "Not that I'm telling you how to do your job…"

"I'll decide when it's a good time," the cop said. "Sir, if you'll come with me…"

"Get off me!" Jake howled, and he pulled hard and out of the man's grip. He ran to the stretcher and pulled the sheet off Tom's head.

"Tom!" He grabbed at his brother's face. "Tom! Wake up! Wake up, bro! We have to finish the doors! We're having dinner tonight with your wife and kids! I can't go by myself, wake up! Wake up! Don't do this! Tom!"

The officer walked toward Jake and the female paramedic held up a hand. The cop stopped, exhaled sharply, and folded his arms over his puffed-out chest.

"Tom," Jake said quietly now. "Tom…we have to get going. You have to come with me now." Tears filled his vision and Tom's face became a distorted, watery picture. "You *can't* do this to me, Tom. You can't do this!"

Then Tom's eyes opened.

Jake caught his breath. "Tom?"

Tom blinked.

Jake turned to the female paramedic. "I told you!" Then he turned toward the cop. "I told you he wasn't dead!"

Tom lunged from the stretcher and gnashed at the arms of the second paramedic. The man shouted in pain as Tom's teeth bit through skin and tissue. The paramedic tried to pull away but Tom's bite was locked on the guy's flesh.

Jake stood in stunned disbelief. "Tom? Wha…what…"

"Somebody help!" the paramedic yelled. "Shoot him! Shoot him for Christ's sake!"

Jake watched as Tom raged like a rabid animal and tore at the paramedic's arm until Jake could see broken veins, tendons and bone. The scene was beyond anything Jake had ever known was physically possible.

Another gunshot rang out; the bullet ripped through Tom's skull and his lifeless jaw released the paramedic's arm.

"No!" Jake yelled.

There were no more gunshots. Only screams of pain and of despair.

"No!"

"Oh my God!" the paramedic panicked. "My fucking arm!"

Jake stared at the paramedic's arm but all he saw was a stump where a hand should have been, along with a torn, bloody limb that resembled a prop from a horror movie. He spun around and saw that the cop that had grabbed him was holding his gun; smoke still emitted from the barrel.

"You shot him…" It was more a statement than a question, uttered as a fuzzy afterthought. The look of shock on the cop's face told Jake that even the officer was surprised he'd pulled the trigger. Suddenly the hazy confusion in Jake's head was pushed out by a fiery anger and all he wanted to do was rip the cop apart, limb by limb. "You son of a bitch!" Jake ran toward the cop. Stunned and scared, the officer lowered the gun to his side. Jake hunched his shoulders forward and barreled into the man at full speed. The two of them slammed violently to the ground and the cop's gun fell out of his hand and skidded along the grass. Jake popped up on his knees and wasted no time delivering punch after savage punch into the man's face, chest and neck. The cop tried to defend with both hands, but any strength he had wasn't about to match the adrenaline-fueled hatred within Jake.

The strange part was that Jake didn't aim for any part of the cop's body in particular. All he did was swing.

And swing again.

He wanted to damage the man that had shot his brother as badly as he physically could, police officer or not.

By the time other officers came to the cop's aid and pulled Jake off, the man's face was a mangled wreck. His eyes were swollen and closed and he appeared unconscious. Jake wasn't sure if the guy was still alive, and he didn't care.

Several officers held Jake tightly and escorted him to a patrol car. Then one of them opened the rear door and another held Jake's head as he calmly lowered himself into the back seat.

"I understand how upset you must be," one of the officers said. "But that wasn't a smart thing to do. Not smart at all."

Jake looked back at the officer that had just spoken. He stared at him absently, and when the officer raised his eyebrows in anticipation of Jake's response, he said nothing. He simply sat in the car and faced forward. Jake even smiled inside a little when he heard the officer scoff angrily while closing the car door.

Jake sat in the back seat alone. His mind, hardly functional, could only manage to replay moments of the last ten minutes; the neighbor stumbling out of his front door, Santa eating the man's guts, his brother getting attacked, and the gunshots…it all blended together into a sort of din. For Jake, it was like staring at a piece of 3-D art, and all he could see was a disorganized array of lines and colors.

A dispatcher's voice came over the police radio on the dashboard, saying something that Jake not only believed, but had half-expected to hear. "All units, we have incidents in progress…claims of an unarmed man biting another man on Wilshire and Hollywood; please respond."

Jake knew the area well. It was on the other side of town. It was hardly a shock to him that the same thing was happening somewhere else. Then the dispatcher continued. "All units, we also have similar incidents on Post Road, Kessler, Merwin, Birch, Snowapple, Chatham and Benjamin Heights; please respond."

*Oh. Wow.*

That last call had woken Jake from his near-catatonic state. From what the dispatcher had said, it seemed like an outbreak of some kind was happening all over town. It didn't occur to Jake that it might also be happening in other towns throughout the state.

He looked out the window of the police car. The entire neighborhood was in pandemonium. People were running in every direction, as if trying to escape from some kind of terror. Jake saw others acting the same way Santa and Tom had, clawing and biting people. It seemed to Jake that the 'crazy' ones, the ones biting and attacking, were chasing the 'normal' people all over the place.

Then Jake saw a familiar face running toward the patrol car—it was the female paramedic. She saw Jake sitting in the back seat and ran to the door. She tried the handle. Nothing. Her eyes met Jake's and he felt an emotion that was somehow foreign to him in that moment: sympathy. She had been the only one who had shown any sympathy toward him during the entire ordeal and he couldn't help but return the feeling.

Jake shook his head, the gesture saying, *The door is locked.*

Then he motioned toward the front. She reached for the driver's door and it opened. Jumping into the driver's seat, she slammed the door and began yelling, *"Where the hell are the keys! We have to get out of here!"* She reached up into the visor, felt under the seat, into the center console, and over the computer that perched on top of a swiveling tray mounted to the dashboard. Then she looked down to the passenger seat.

A set of keys. Luckily, the officer had been lazy and had tossed them there upon arriving on scene.

"Find 'em?" Jake asked. His voice floated calmly in a comatose-like manner.

"Are you sick or something?" she asked him point blank as she spun around in the driver's seat to face him. "Because if you are sick, I'll kick your ass out of this car right now!"

Jake stared into her eyes, as if deep in thought, then said, "No. I feel fine."

"You sure? Did you get attacked or something? Because whatever's going around could be airborne or it could be transferred by bodily fluids. Think; I need you to be sure."

Again Jake paused, then nodded.

The paramedic took a deep breath, then said, "Okay."

She flipped through the keys until she found one with a car logo on it and slid it into the ignition. The engine roared to life and she quickly shifted the transmission into 'drive.' Then she pushed the pedal to the floor and the car jumped forward.

It was only seconds later that the car was already half a mile away from the maelstrom that had taken over the neighborhood. Jake looked up into the rearview mirror and caught the paramedic glancing out the back window more than once.

"Where are we going?" he asked.

"Um…I don't know."

Jake took a few seconds, as if reflecting on her words before saying softly, "Sounds good to me."

In the mirror, her eyes finally met his.

"I *am* sorry, you know."

He looked deep into those blue eyes again. "I know. Thank you."

Her eyes focused back to the road, but not before he had enough time to see small pools begin to fill up the bottoms of her reddened eyelids. Surely the emotion on display wasn't for him. Was it? That would be impossible. She'd only just met him minutes ago and she didn't even know his name. It was probably for a boyfriend or husband, maybe even a family member or members. Still, it was nice to see such a reaction. Amid all the chaos, he'd somehow managed to get away safely with a warm, caring person.

They would do well to stick together, he thought, as they drove on without direction or a destination.

He couldn't help but look at all the houses decorated with holiday decorations, everything from plastic Santas to light-up reindeers, to wreaths of all sizes. But behind that holiday cheer was something else. Something sinister. And as sounds of screams, sirens and gunshots filtered into the squad car, Jake knew that with so much already having happened, such as the death of his brother, whatever had contaminated the world on this holy of days was far from over.

It was the first day of the apocalypse.

# THE REIGN OF DEER

JASON MOOERS

The snow was wild, crosshatching its way to the ground. It clung to the edges of his long white hair as he tightened his coat. He let out a frosty sigh as he headed towards the clanging alarm.

Piercing through the winter air, the bell rang. Small figures ran quickly through the snow on either side of the large man with tasks of their own. Everyone knew the drill, but the big man needed to make sure. He needed to see what had really happened.

The ominous dark shape of the stable came into view. The cold and lifeless feeling chilled the large man to the core; one of the barn doors slowly creaked back and forth by the wild snow. There was only darkness beyond the door.

The man sighed and brushed the frost from his brow. He shoved the door open, letting the light from behind him cascade inside.

He stood in shock, pumping his fists in frustration. "They got everyone. Every blasted last one of them!" The large man wanted to punch something.

Two small men moved to his side.

"We'll clean immediately!" they announced with squeaking voices. They were carrying mops, shovels, and buckets.

The big man allowed them inside. He turned back into the harsh snow and hollered to the others, "Did anyone see which way they went?"

One small volunteer stopped and ran to the large man. "They went south."

"Well, no shit." The large man placed his hands on his hips. He couldn't make out who was speaking to him in the dark, snowy weather, but most of these fellas looked exactly the same. "Which way?"

The little man pointed off in one direction.

The big man smiled, and then tossed his informant aside. "Someone get my gear! We have to move fast!"

The little people scurried like cockroaches. One carried a large, double-barreled shotgun toward the large man.

He took it and rested it on his shoulder. "This will be no silent night!"

*　*　*

Jackie was always the fastest. She stopped to listen. At first all she could hear was her own breath, but soon the clumsy footfall of her companions and their idle banter reassured her that she hadn't lost them yet. She smiled and leaned against an old tree whose roots tried to trip her up.

Jackie was a raven-haired girl, young and fit. Her hazel eyes were always alert as she scanned around the wilderness, keeping an eye out for moose, bear, or anything that could be a threat. Her skin was unusually pale for someone who loved the outdoors as much as she did. The cold air kept her cheeks and nose bright red. She laughed as she listened to her friends complain as they drew closer.

"Where the hell did Jackie go?"

"She never waits. Just keep following her footprints."

"That girl's a pain in the ass."

"I'd like to give her a pain in the ass."

"This your first time?"

"Yeah, why?"

"Good luck with that."

"Ain't we far enough yet?"

"Depends if you're a bunch of wusses, or if you came out here for some real adventure," Jackie said and smiled at her companions as they entered the thicket.

At the head of the pack was George. "Easy there, Jackie," he scolded her from under his fur-lined hood. "We've been hiking for nearly half a day." He smiled at his life-long friend through his bushy-red beard. His new look reminded Jackie of a red Paul Bunyan.

"Yeah. And this shit ain't light." Russel happily dropped his large pack to the ground. He stood and stretched. He was a tall man with dark curly hair that leaked out from under his wool cap and danced across his dark eyes. This was his first time camping with the troupe, although he didn't seem to have the stomach for it. The flight they took to get here made the man lose his lunch. He seemed miserable about the whole camping experience. Jackie had no idea why he was here.

"Oh goodie. Are we camping here?" Nisha led the cluster of stragglers as they entered the clearing. Her large, gold earrings sparkled and dangled out of each side of her hood. Jackie never understood why she would wear jewelry out on these trips.

Following her were Steve, the pilot, Jenna, Bobby and Barney. Jackie counted her troops. "Eight. That's everyone, right?"

George counted in his head for a moment. "Yeah. We're all here." The campers were pleased to be dropping their packs into the crunching snow.

Jackie leaned in to George. "We're not there yet, George. I got a place far less boring in mind."

George nodded and said to the group, "Take ten, everyone. Eat something and we'll get moving."

"What's wrong with staying here?" Russel moaned. "The further away we go, the further we have to walk back to the plane! We're already out in the middle of nowhere. Hell, where the plane landed was good enough. We could have camped there. It's all frozen trees, snow and dirt. It all looks the same!"

"Calm down, Russel," George said. "We're almost there. Right, Jackie?"

Jackie was annoyed, but she did her best to smile and nod.

Bobby sat next to Jackie. "Where are you taking us this time?" Bobby had camped out in these hills more times than anyone. He was the one that had showed this whole forest to Jackie. He had salt and pepper hair and a five o'clock shadow that never went away. He smelled like Old Spice.

Jackie spoke in a hushed tone. "The hill over the glacier; I want everyone to see how amazing it is," Jackie said in a hushed tone

"That's about three hours from here. It'll be dark before we get there." Bobby kept his voice down. He didn't want to let everyone know they weren't as close as George had led them to believe.

"I know they can do it." Jackie's mind was made up, and once that happened, no one could change it. Bobby shook his head.

"Nice landing, Steve!" Bobby decided to change the subject.

Steve smiled and nodded as he sipped some steaming soup from his thermos.

"That was your smoothest yet!" Bobby added.

"Not smooth enough for some people!" Jenna burst in. She laughed wildly between her mittens. Her wavy hair danced around her freckled face as she glanced at Russel. His eyebrows were in angry mode. Jenna pantomimed throwing up between giggles.

Russel bit his lower lip as he stood up.

"Russel!" George interjected. "Relax. Jenna, that's enough. We all have to get along, okay? It's going to be a long trip if you keep snapping at each other's throats."

Bobby knew that the attitudes of the group were only going to get worse the longer the hike took, so he ended the break. "Come on, guys." He threw his bags back over his shoulders. "The sooner we get there, the sooner we can get a fire going and relax."

"Yes, good idea." George got everyone back on their feet. The last one up was Russel, who was grumbling to himself.

Jackie once again took the lead as they ventured off into the icy wilderness.

* * *

It was dark before the campers reached their destination and Jackie had already begun fire preparations before everyone had arrived to the site. Russel, surprisingly silent, brought up the rear. Although it was dark, Jackie knew just where they were. They were on a clearing beside a cliff overlooking a glacier she expected everyone to 'ooh' and 'ahh' about when the sun came up.

The clearing offered a safe place to camp; there were no looming branches to catch fire. The sky was clear and filled with stars. Even the moon offered the campers some light as they collected wood for the fire. Jackie was quick with an axe and accumulated more wood than all of her troop combined.

One side of the camp seemed to drop off into utter darkness.

"Be careful over there," Bobby remarked. "It's a long drop." He didn't want to say more and ruin Jackie's surprise in the morning.

Once the fire was burning and the four tents were pitched, everyone was gratefully settling down. Even Jackie seemed satisfied with their work and relaxed for the first time since they'd landed almost eight hours ago.

Steve was checking his GPS to make sure the plane was still where he'd left it. Russel sat down next to him with a thud and said, "Lovely patch of trees you've found here. Looks a lot like a place we were at *seven hours* ago!"

Steven glanced up from the glowing GPS screen. "What's your problem? We're here, aren't we?"

"We still gotta walk back!" Russel groaned as he looked around the campfire. When his eyes landed on Jackie, he sighed. If there was any chance of getting into that woman's pants, he was going to have to stop his belly aching. He was going to have to cheer up, no matter how many blisters he could feel burning inside his boots.

Jenna giggled and said, "You don't have to walk back. Stay here."

Russel looked at Jenna. She was a cute girl, and she had freckles, which Russel adored. But she was a flake, and Russel knew for a fact that she had shared more than a sleeping bag with most everyone sitting around the fire. Russel thought, *If I can't get closer to Jackie, I could use Jenna to keep warm.*

He gazed across the campfire at the other girl in their party, Nisha. She was Indian, or Hindu, or something similar that Russel didn't care about. She was an ethnic chick, and he saw that she had eyes for George. She couldn't keep her hands off him. She would reach out and touch him with any excuse she could think of. Russel had told George about her affection back in college, but George didn't seem to care. He looked at Nisha as more of a sister.

Jackie was the girl every man around the fire wanted. She was beautiful, and unattainable, and that made every one of them want her even more. Bobby had camped with her for years before anyone else, and there were rumors flying around through college that he was her *older* lover. But after getting to know Bobby over the past day or so, Russel doubted it. Looking at the group around the fire, Russel assumed none of them knew the warmth of Jackie's energetic body. She was his mission, and so far he was failing miserably.

"Maybe I will stay here." Russel changed his tone. "If this place is as beautiful as you say it is, Jackie, I just might stay. You'd come visit, wouldn't you?" His smile was returned to him and then

Jackie turned her attention to the potatoes that were packed into the red hot coals of the fire.

A pot of chili began to simmer over the flames as the night waged on. The moon slowly sank behind the trees, letting sinister shadows consume the land around the camp.

Barney and Jenna were busy smoking and passing joints amongst the campers. Jenna began to giggle even more. Barney, who barely ever spoke a word, coughed into his hand with every puff.

"Jesus, Barney!" Jenna mocked. "It ain't like the first time you've taken a drag! You smoke like my grandma!"

George pulled the boiling chili from the fire. "How hungry are you guys?" He began to dish out the pot into mugs and pass them around.

"I'm freakin' starving!" Jenna exclaimed as she took a bite and burned her mouth.

"Chill out, lady. It's hot." Bobby tossed a beer across the circle to Jenna. She nodded a thank you as she doused her burning lips and tongue with the cold ale.

"So why did you bring us out this far anyway?" Russel moved in on Jackie.

"You'll see in the morning." Jackie didn't even glance at Russel as she carefully cooled her spoonfuls of chili before eating.

Russel was aroused by her blowing lips.

"So you're George's friend?" she asked.

"Yeah, we roomed together in school."

Jackie nodded and went back to eating. Russel made several efforts to get a conversation going, but Jackie was intent on eating and ended each topic abruptly.

After dinner, sleeping arrangements were made.

Nisha insisted on sleeping with George in his tent, like always. George didn't care. He'd consumed several drinks and was ready for a deep sleep. Nisha would end up lying awake all night, hoping George would wake up horny, perhaps from a dirty dream, and pounce. It was her routine.

Jenna had tagged her coughing pot supplier, Barney, for the evening. The two of them were thoroughly drunk and probably wouldn't remember if anything did or didn't happen in the morning.

Bobby went to one tent without even talking with anyone. He didn't care who else shared his tent. He was going to sleep, so his orders were to be left alone…on penalty of death.

Russel sat at the dying fire with Jackie and Steve. He tried to mind-will Steve into sharing a tent with Bobby. Russel was exhausted, and conversation had led nowhere. This was his only chance.

Jackie was the first to stand up.

She pinched her fingers on the sides of her nose and took a deep breath. "All right, gentlemen. I'll take first watch." She got up and carried her heavy blanket to the edge of the clearing.

Steve glanced up from his glowing GPS screen and smiled. "Righty oh. See you in the morning!" He rose and wandered into the empty tent.

Russel sat alone by the deep red embers, his eyes burning from the smoke. He was in so much pain from all the physical work he wasn't used to. Plus, the cold made his joints ache. Part of him wanted to sleep but the other part wanted to see what Jackie was up to.

*   *   *

Jackie sat along the edge of the wilderness. It was her favorite place to be. She knew her companions liked to camp, but for her, it was sheer love. She loved the smells, sounds, and sights all around her. She loved to share it with her friends, but knew none of them would ever understand what it meant to her. This was where she was free from everything. There were no bills or collection calls. There were no bosses to answer to. Jackie simply adored being left alone.

"Hello." Russel made her jump as he approached.

"Jesus, Russel. What?" So much for her alone time.

"I just thought you could use some company." He took an un-welcomed seat next to her. "I couldn't sleep anyway."

"Why are you here, Russel?" She stared out into the opaque blackness of the woods.

"I told you. I couldn't sleep."

"Not that. Why did you come camping?" She hiked her collar up over her cheeks a little. "You obviously don't like hiking. You bitch about the cold. You couldn't even stomach the plane ride. I get that you're friends with George. We all are. He's got tons of friends, but most of them don't want to go camping in this part of Canada."

"Okay, you want the truth?" He sighed. "My parents both used to hike out here when they were young. When they got older they'd never take me. Never! So when I heard that George took these little trips, I knew I had to go. Just to spite them."

"You're full of shit." Jackie didn't believe a word of his story. "What's your last name?"

"It's Blank."

"Blank? I'll have to check with Bobby in the morning. He knows everyone who's camped out this way for decades now."

"Well, maybe they didn't camp exactly here. But I know it was somewhere near here. He might not have…"

"Shhh!" Jackie cut him off and leaned forward, straining her eyes and ears.

"Well, I know that if they were here they'd be able to tell you…"

"Shut up!" She stood and took a few steps away from Russel. "Something's watching us. I can feel it."

"Right now, I'm watching you. And let me tell you, it's a welcome sight." He hoped that wasn't too forward.

It went unnoticed.

"I think it's a moose, or maybe a deer."

"Then make some noise and it should run away." Russel grabbed the chili pot and proceeded to beat it with a large spoon. "Get out of here!"

"Damn you, Russel! Shut up!" Jackie grabbed the pot from him and momentarily thought of beating him over the head with it. "If it is a moose, they can be territorial. This isn't our land, you idiot."

"Wh…what's going on?" Steve popped his head out of the tent. "Is it a bear?"

Other people began to stir in their tents.

"I'm sorry, guys. Russel's just being an alarmist. It was just a moose or deer or something."

Suddenly, the sky erupted with a strange howling sound. Jackie had never heard anything like it before. It sounded like the scream of a wounded deer, only much stronger, and with a deeper overtone.

Russel was about to speak, but Jackie struck him with the pot, knocking him into the snow. The guy was really getting on her nerves. "Learn to shut up," she muttered.

The howl filled the sky, making it almost near impossible to tell where it was coming from.

Steve grabbed his jacket and went to Jackie's side. "That ain't a moose or a deer," he said.

Then the howl was joined by another. They called to each other in a way that made Jackie's skin crawl. Her body shivered in sweat as she scanned the trees, searching for the creatures calling each other.

"Is that a wolf?" Nisha had joined Steve and Jackie.

"It's nothing I've ever heard before." Steve wiped and reapplied his glasses.

"I think there's another." A third call joined in and grew in volume. The howls resonated like there were cows directly from Hell descending upon the camp. "And another." Jackie picked up her firewood axe and never took her eyes off the woods. The howls were getting closer, but nothing came into view. "Nisha, get George. Tell him to get his gun. Hurry!"

Nisha was lost in the sounds, and didn't even know anyone was talking to her until Steve nudged her. She scrambled back to her tent like a child running up the cellar stairs, positive that something was chasing her. "George, wake up you sleepy bastard!" she said.

The howls grew in number and drowned out any conversations going on around Jackie. Bobby hadn't emerged from his tent. Barney and Jenna stuck their heads out of theirs, and then retreated within to find some clothes.

George burst to life, jumping from his tent to Jackie's side. His 'just-in-case' rifle in hand. "What is it?"

"Don't know. I don't see anything!" Jackie replied.

Nisha scrambled back out of the tent with the flashlight and hoped to God it was charged. She turned it on, blinding everyone in the camp until she calmed down enough to point it out into the woods. It cast wild and twisting shadows through the bushes and trees, shining off the ice and snow, almost blinding the group.

Jackie grabbed the spinning flashlight from Nisha and slowly scanned the woods with it. "I'd say there are at least five," she said. George and Jackie slowly scanned the woods. Whatever was howling sounded like it was right upon them.

George noticed Russel in the snow. "He all right?"

"He's fine." Jackie kicked him and he stirred and muttered to himself.

A sudden crash from behind made Jackie, Steve, George, and Nisha spin around. Something had crashed into a tent. Pieces of camping equipment went flying in every direction. Something snarled and howled as it shredded the tent. Jenna and Barney both screamed from inside.

"What the hell is that?" Steve hollered.

George aimed his rifle, trying to see his target through the scope. He was about to pull the trigger when an underwear-clad Jenna came flying through the chaos toward them. She fell into the snow, wailing and sobbing. Steve ran ahead to reach her. George lifted his rifle.

"Get her out of the way!" Jackie ordered.

"What about Barney?" Jenna wailed as Steve dragged her through the snow to the group.

Barney's yell thundered through the chaos as another beastly shape seemed to appear out of nowhere to join the first in shredding through the camp.

"Barney!" Jenna called. Suddenly the massive shapes, the shredded tent, and Barney all disappeared.

For a moment, everyone was silent. Even the howling ended. The only sound was Jenna sobbing.

"The cliff!" Jackie had just realized what had happened. "They fell over the cliff!"

"Wait here, you guys, and someone wake up Bobby for Christ's sake!" George took control as he and Jackie slowly inched their way towards the mess the creatures had made and the cliff.

"There's a lot of blood, Jackie." George didn't want the rest of the group to hear him.

"I know." Jackie kept the flashlight pointed at the edge of the cliff, where the snow had been scraped away and the tent had been dragged over.

"I think these are some kind of hoof prints," George said.

"I know." Jackie slowed down as they approached the cliff. "Stop looking around and keep that gun ready." She reaffirmed the axe in her hand and together they both peered over the edge. The flashlight revealed the dark silhouette of a tent down below among the ice.

"Do you see a moose or a dear?" George strained his eyes. It was quite a drop. Nothing should have survived a fall like that.

"No. I don't see Barney either." There were only empty shreds of canvas and tattered camping supplies below. They scanned the icy floor and saw nothing else. Not even blood.

"They're gone." George took a step back from the cliff.

"What the hell is wrong with you all? Dragging me out of bed when…" Bobby ended his rant after emerging from his tent when he looked about the campsite. Supplies were scattered everywhere. Steve and Nisha were getting Jenna wrapped in warmer clothing. Russel was sprawled out next to the smoldering fire pit, slowly moaning. "What the hell?"

Jackie didn't have time for explanations. "Something has attacked the campsite, Bobby. Nothing we've ever seen. They took Barney. We don't know where they went."

"Wait." Bobby put his fingers to his temple. "What attacked the campsite?"

"We don't know." George began collecting supplies.

"I think it had antlers." Steve added.

"Was it a crazed moose?" Bobby didn't quite understand. "It's nowhere near mating season."

Slowly, on the wind, came a familiar and haunting howl.

"That's what it is!" Jackie began using the light again.

"Are they're coming back for more?" Nisha helped pull Jenna to her feet.

The sound grew louder as more additional howls once again joined in.

Bobby grabbed the flashlight from Jackie and began stepping towards the woods. "That isn't any moose I've ever heard. It's kind of like a deer in pain, only much worse. How many of them are there?"

"I don't know, but they're getting closer."  The sound grew loud, fast. Everyone huddled together.

Bobby grabbed Jackie by the shoulder. "Did you see them come in from the woods? Because that sound isn't coming from the woods."

"We didn't see them at all until they attacked Barney's tent."

Bobby laughed. "That sound ain't coming from the woods. It's coming from the sky!"

Jackie was thrown back into the group as something large and furry crashed down onto Bobby, who began to yell, and then was suddenly silenced. The flashlight spun across the campsite. Jackie dove for it and spun the beam back at the creature.

The monster turned and stared right back into the light. It was a giant deer, easily the size of a moose. Its fur was silver and black. A huge rack of antlers sprang from its head. Its eyes were dark and hollow. Blood ran down its mouth and along its silver chest. It held Bobby's lifeless body down against the ground with a mighty front hoof. It turned away from the light and proceeded to eat at Bobby's flesh.

"Kill it!" someone shrieked.

There was a crack from George's rifle and the creature yelped, spitting bits of Bobby across his tent. The creature turned back to George and gave him a hard look, as if he was next.

George felt the terror of the creature's stare and stepped back, tripping over Russel and falling back into the snow. The creature turned back and grabbed Bobby with its gore-ridden teeth. Blood ran from the creature's shoulder where it had been shot. It picked up the body and turned towards the campers.

"Shoot it in the head, asshole!" Jackie screamed.

Suddenly, four more of the giant deer creatures descended from above onto the wounded one. They kicked and stomped into the creature, tearing at its flesh with their teeth. They fought among each other as they pulled parts of the wounded deer's body free. Then two more came down to join the fray. One grabbed Bobby's shredded body and the other five collected the parts of the now deceased first killer deer. Then they all took off in unison into the sky, leaving only the soaking red snow behind.

Jackie scanned the sky for the creatures. But once again, they were gone.

"They're going to eat us all!" Jenna sobbed as Nisha embraced her.

"You bitch. What the hell?" Russel hissed at Jackie as he came to, still lying in the snow.

"Get up!" George said and kicked Russel. "Whatever the hell happened to you, I'm sure you deserved it. We don't have time for your bullshit right now."

"What are we going to do if they come back?" Nisha was pushing away freezing tears from her cheeks.

Jackie handed the flashlight back to Nisha. "We're not going to be here if they do. Steve, can you guide us at night back to the plane?"

"Sure can." He fumbled in his pocket and produced his GPS.

"Grab only what you need, everyone," she instructed. "We're leaving, *now!*"

* * *

Jackie and Steve led the party with flashlights and lanterns. Behind them was George with Nisha, who were assisting the still severely-rattled, but relatively-unharmed, Jenna. And following up in the back was Russel. George carried his rifle, with his ammo box in his pocket. Russel carried a pistol he had decided to bring on the trip as an afterthought, and kept an eye to the sky. Jackie hadn't released her axe yet.

There was no complaining about the hike this time. They had opted to leave any heavy equipment behind. Speed was the best option. Russel kept thinking to himself that if everyone had listened to him to begin with, they would already be on their way home. Instead, he got to witness two friends getting slaughtered, and receive a lump the size of a baseball, which was giving him a splitting headache. "Fuck you, Jackie," he muttered to himself.

The woods were eerily quiet. Russel was no expert, but he knew there should be the sounds of creatures other than giant, man-eating deer, in the thick of the wilderness. It was as if nature herself had gone into hiding. He decided to speak up.

"Hey, shouldn't there be animals around? You know. Birds chirping? Wolves? Anything? We've been at this all day and night and I ain't even seen a goddamn squirrel."

"They must know something we didn't," George sighed.

"Something *you* didn't. I wanted to stay by the plane," Russel said under his breath.

"Hold!" Jackie said suddenly as she held her fist in the air. Everyone froze. Russel tried to listen for the howling. But he couldn't hear anything beyond his own breath.

"Wait," she commanded and walked ahead.

"Since when is she in charge?" Russel grumbled.

George heard him. "Since she's the most experienced with wilderness survival. Just keep your gun ready and your negative mouth shut."

"What'd he say?" Nisha leaned in.

"Nothing important." George looked up as Jackie returned.

She grabbed Steve and drew the crowd together in a huddle. In a hushed tone Jackie said, "Someone else is around. I saw human prints. They were fresh. I don't know who it is but if someone is wandering alone at night out here, it either means they're crazy or they have friends somewhere nearby. Either way, we're better off being left alone all the way back to the plane. So keep it quiet."

They began to move along again. *Great,* Russel thought. *Not only do we have killer deer to contend with. There may be some psychopath out there hunting us down. Can this night get any better?*

Right on cue, the howling began again. It sounded distant, but it still sent the worst chills down everyone's spines.

"Shit, let's move!" Jackie picked up the pace as the party began to run in a new direction. "Some polar caves are close. If we can make it there and find one, we may be safe for a while."

The more howling they heard, the faster they ran, and the faster they ran, the closer the howling sounded. Russel was afraid to even look into the sky as they ran. It would only slow him down, and if he tripped, he felt like he'd be as good as dead. All he could do was run as fast as he could and hope nothing would get in his way.

But something did get in his way. A large killer deer crashed down right behind Jackie and Steve and turned its attention to George, Jenna, and Nisha, who were running right toward it.

"Jackie!" George hollered and fired his rifle towards the beast. It didn't even flinch as the bullet zipped by its head. Its vast black and silver coating of fur waved in the breeze. Blood and gore matted around its snarling teeth and entrails dripped from its chin. The deer had eyes of black, soulless coal, and they were fixed on George and the two women.

"How'd you miss, you asshole? The thing's bigger than your car?" Russel said and started running towards his friend and the girls. Before he could even think of pointing his gun, he tripped and fell face first into the snow.

There were two more thuds as a pair of deer landed on either side of George. He fumbled in a pocket, trying to collect more ammo. It scattered about in the snow as the three deer advanced on them. Jenna shrieked as one grabbed her with its teeth by the arm and flung her away from the others. But before she could even get back to her feet, another landed and grabbed her by the face, digging its vicious teeth right into her skull. She screamed into its mouth, and with the closing of its jaw, was instantly silenced.

The first deer lowered its horns and ran right into George, sending him flying over Russel, who chose to lie as still and as dead-like as he possibly could. When George crashed into a tree some twenty feet back, the deer pursued him, leaping over Russel. The second deer followed, stepping mere inches away from Russel's head. Russel almost yelled, but was terrified at bringing attention to himself.

The third deer that was in front of Russel stopped and looked down at the man. It licked its chops and wagged its tail as it approached the possum.

Russel closed his eyes and waited for the impending doom.

But before the deer could attack, there was a loud *crack*, and something wet and hot splattered over Russel. Nisha was standing with tears in her eyes. George's rifle was in her hands as smoke curled from the barrel. She had blown the skull of the killer deer wide open, and its headless body collapsed with a crunch next to

Russel. Its death was much more convincing than Russel playing possum.

Nisha sobbed uncontrollably as Russel got to his feet. Before he could even say anything to her, he saw another deer touch down near Jackie, who swung her axe and began to run. She bolted into the woods with the thunderous monster at her heels.

Russel pushed Nisha aside and ran after them.

* * *

Before Steve even knew what was happening, Jackie shoved him aside and went face to face with one of the monstrous creatures.

"You have to live, Steve. You're our only way out of here! Head for the caves! I'll find you there!" She ran, and the deer followed.

Steve surveyed the battlefield. One deer was dead in the center. Nisha stood by it, dropping the rifle into the snow. Another deer was ripping apart what could only have been Jenna. Two other deer were playing wishbone with George.

"There's not going to be anyone left to save." He knew Jackie was right. He had to make it or no one would. He was afraid to call out to Nisha and draw unwanted attention from the monster, so he stood eagerly waiting for her to turn toward him.

"Well, they'll be on the naughty list for sure," a voice rumbled from behind Steve. He gasped and turned around to see a large man standing with his hands on his hips. He wore a deep green winter coat and a black stocking cap over his white curly hair and beard. He also wore what appeared to be a set of shop goggles. He reached around his back and pulled out the largest double-barrel shotgun Steve had ever seen.

Without a moment's hesitation, he walked down into the field.

"Duck, girl," he commanded to Nisha as he fired, causing one creature to explode. "One." He reloaded and cocked his gun at almost supernatural speed. He fired at the other creature that was enjoying the remains of George. "Two." The third one that was chewing on Jenna had her bra stuck in its teeth. It snarled and ran as fast as it could at the large, bearded man.

It exploded all across the snowy field and blood dripped from the trees. "Three." He began walking back toward Steve and grabbed Nisha and George's rifle on the way. "Nice job, darling. That's four." He nodded in approval at the dead deer he stepped over.

Nisha seemed to be at her wits end. She sobbed uncontrollably. He kept trying to hand her the rifle, but she was in no state of mind to notice.

As he walked back up to Steve, he squeezed deer guts from his beard. "Well, Steve, suck it up and be a man. We're not done yet I'm afraid." Steve realized he had never told the man his name. "Is that the only one you killed?"

"Uh… no. One at our camp, too." Steve felt like he was in a daze.

"That's five." The large man pressed his gloved finger to the side of his nose, and with a nod, blew his runny nose into the snow. "Are there any more foolish campers out here?"

"Um, yeah. That way, sir." Steve pointed in the direction Jackie had run.

"Then let's go." The big man swung his rifle back over his shoulder. He ushered Steve and the sobbing Nisha along. "I'm no sir, Steve. Call me Kris."

* * *

Jackie ran with all her might, hearing the thing snorting and running behind her. She intentionally ran through the thickest brush she could find, letting its antlers get tangled again and again. She knew it was faster than her, so she had to be smarter. The night was ending and thankfully she could see her path through the snow.

She wondered who was still alive. Amidst the chaos, she couldn't tell. She hoped and prayed for all of them as she raced along like a wild rabbit with a starving fox on its heels. She hoped for everyone's sake that Steve had made it.

The trees were thinning out and the polar caves were approaching. She was going to have to run faster than she ever had before to make it into a cave before the beast overtook her.

She could feel the monster's hideous breath on her neck as she ran with all her might. She could feel the thud of its hooves by her heels as she dove into the first cave she saw. There was a crashing and scraping sound as the walls of the cave interfered with the beast's antlers. It wasn't a deep hole. She pressed her back against the wall to face the snarling, howling beast before her.

Quickly, its pungent odor of wet dog and rotting flesh permeated the air. It began twisting its head to find ways of inching further and further into the cave. The deer obsessively licked the gore from its teeth as it wheezed and snarled at Jackie.

Its hooves dug furiously into the soil as it continued to slowly reach its prey.

Jackie realized it was going to get her. This cave didn't narrow quite enough to ensure her safety. She wished she hadn't dropped that axe. As the beast inched its way forward, she could feel its damp breath on her face. Then she closed her eyes, awaiting the inevitable. She felt its tongue licking at her cheek.

Then a loud gunshot filled the interior of the cave.

Jackie tried to open her eyes, but they were blinded by blood. "Hello?" She didn't know who had just saved her, but someone had just shot the creature dead.

"Jackie, are you all right?"

It was the one voice Jackie wasn't thrilled to hear. But it was still better than being deer food.

"Russel, yeah, I'm okay. What happened? Where is everyone?"

"They're good. They're safe. We got into a cave like you said. I heard all the noise. Let's get you out of there."

As the beast sank down onto the cave floor, Jackie was able to climb over it. The morning was fast approaching. The sky was turning orange and cloud stripes stretched along the horizon. Russel handed Jackie a rag once she'd stepped out. He was also coated in what Jackie hoped was deer and not human blood.

"Sorry about the mess," he smiled. She tried to mop the stink off her to the best of her ability.

"Thanks for the rescue. I owe you one."

"Yeah." Russel nodded and led Jackie towards the polar caves.

"So everyone's okay?" She was thrilled.

"Some bites and scratches. Nothing we can't handle." He was careful not to make eye contact with her as they wandered around some large rocks. He kept an eye to the sky.

"That was fast. How'd they get away?"

Russel gave her a huge smile. "The deer all ran after you."

"Wow."

"Yep, you saved us all." Russel chose a cave and led Jackie inside.

* * *

The cave turned to the left. Jackie walked around the corner and saw no one. She turned back just as Russel put his gun to her head.

"Like you said, you owe me now, you little bitch." He shoved her against the wall. "This is all your fault. You lured me here with your sexy ways! I wouldn't have come. I hate camping! I hate flying! God, I hate all those annoying people you call friends."

He pressed the gun tight against her cheek. The outside of the gun was cold, but the inside was still hot.

"You wanted to know why I came on this trip? I wanted you! I don't give a shit about any of the rest of it. Hell, I don't think there's a way out for us at this point. But if I'm gonna die here, at least I'll get what I came here for!" He thrust his hand into her coat and began to fish around through the layers until he found skin. "Ooh, there you are. You feel so warm." He slid his icy fingers up under her bra.

This was the moment when Jackie realized she would rather take a bullet in her head than give a creep like Russel any kind of satisfaction. She had friends out there in real trouble. So with all her might, she swung her knee up as hard as she could.

She felt something hard crunch against her kneecap and Russel yelped in pain. She grabbed his face with one hand and shoved him hard into the stone wall. Then she removed his wandering hand from her clothing with the other. The gun wasn't a factor. Russel was instantly out, again.

"Looks like you're on your own, buddy." She took the gun and left him unconscious in the cave. "I hope that hurts as much as I think it will when you wake up, you sick bastard."

When she stepped out of the cave, a giant shadow loomed over her and a wet dog smell filled her nostrils. She dove into a small opening under some rocks adjacent to the cave. She couldn't see it from where she was, but she was pretty sure it was another of the killer deer…and this one was even larger than the others.

She held her breath and listened. It was smelling the air. Perhaps it smelled the deer blood soaked into her clothing, or perhaps it smelled her. If they could track prey, that would explain how the group was followed once everyone had left the camp.

With each footfall, the deer made the earth quake. Then an enormous hoof stepped into Jackie's limited view. It was just outside her little cave. The sniffing grew louder and Jackie could feel the air flowing in and out of the cave with each sniff. A second later, giant teeth came into view as red mucus dripped onto the rocks. The creature's mouth was mere inches away. If the thing was as big as Jackie feared, the pistol would only piss it off, unless she could get it right between the eyes. But from where she was, the best she could do was shoot it in the foot. The space was too small to move without exposing an arm or leg.

Seconds passed like hours as the giant beast smelled the woman who was too frightened to move.

"Jackie!" a voice screamed from the cave. Russel was waking up, and he sounded like he was in agonizing pain. The teeth vanished from Jackie's view. "You whore, Jackie!" The hoof stepped away from the hole she was hiding in. Regaining some courage, she inched closer to get a better view.

The creature was enormous. Now that the sun was rising, she could see more detail. It looked like an enormous reindeer with matted fur, tufts of it ripped out to expose its hide. This one was indeed bigger than the ones Jackie had already seen. It stood about twenty five feet tall with antlers any hunter would have envied and wanted to mount on a very large wall. Its hair was almost all silver, blotched with blood and filth. Jackie couldn't see its face. It was looking into the cave.

Russel crawled into sight. As soon as the creature saw him, it began to tear at the entrance, ripping the stone from the mountain face and tossing it aside. It was going to pull the side of the mountain apart to reach him.

For once Russel didn't have something to say. He simply cried and sat like a lump. He melted into a five-year-old who was waiting for his punishment. As much as Jackie despised Russel, she still didn't want to see him die. Besides, she did owe him.

She climbed out of the hole and hollered at the beast to get it to turn around. "Hey, Frankenbeast!"

The creature's head spun around to see its dinner standing there, throwing insults. This one's eyes were the most demonic of all the deer. One eye was a dark black color, but the other was like a pearl, with deep blue veins bulging throughout. It had a gash in its left nostril. Mucus seeped out as it snarled hungrily at Jackie.

"That's right, bitch. I'm over here!" she yelled.

It took a few thunderous steps forward and lowered its head down to Jackie.

"That's right. Be the stupid animal that you are." Jackie slowly raised the gun and pointed it right between the dumb creature's eyes.

"Like a deer caught in headlights," she smirked.

But instead of the report of he gun, all she heard was a dull *click*. There were no bullets left.

* * *

The creature's mouth opened so large that Jackie felt as if she could be swallowed whole. She braced herself for the end, once again.

But then a loud booming filled the air and she was sprayed with a fresh coat of deer blood. Half of the monster's skull was wide open and brain bits clung to everything within fifteen feet of it. The giant creature fell back against the cave entrance with a thud, causing the destroyed cave to collapse in on itself, trapping anything left inside.

Jackie stood still, dripping with blood. She was red from head to toe.

"Nice color. I like it," a large, bearded man said as he waltzed up the pathway. He brought along Steve and Nisha. Jackie was so relieved to see them that she ran and stumbled down the mountain into Steve's arms.

"You guys made it!" she cried.

"You too." Steve hugged the bloody girl.

"Awfully brave of you, little Jacklynn, having a face to face with Olive, the other reindeer." The big man holstered his shotgun.

"This is Kris. He's going to get us to our plane safely," Steve smiled.

Kris looked around at the mess and shook his head. "If this is everyone, we should be off." Kris didn't say another word as he whisked the survivors through the snow. They heard no more howls and saw no more snarling deer. In the daylight it almost seemed like a horrible dream. But anyone glancing at Jackie's bloody silhouette was reminded it most definitely was not a dream.

They reached the plane in a few hours. Steve was very happy to see his friend, and he petted the fuselage affectionately. Then he helped the silent Nisha climb onboard.

Before Jackie boarded, she stopped. "Hold on a minute. What the hell?" She couldn't live with herself if she didn't know what had happened. She turned to glare at Kris. "You know what happened, so fess up, mister!"

Steve climbed from the cockpit and stood next to his friend.

The man eyed Jackie from head to toe and scowled at her. "Do you believe in Santa Claus?"

Jackie chuckled to herself. "No. That's for kids."

Without a word, the large man leveled his massive gun and shot her to smithereens. Before all the pieces had a chance to come to rest on the plane, he turned to Steve and asked him the same question. "Little Steven, do you believe in Santa Claus?"

"Yes!" Steve was in shock.

"Good. I have no tolerance for unbelievers," Kris said. "I don't suppose I can get a ride home?"

Steve wasn't about to argue with the man. "Anywhere you need to go."

"Just head north. We'll get there."

* * *

"You see," Kris explained. "Everyone knows that Santa needs a team of eight flying reindeer to pull his sleigh. But the flying reindeer had become infertile after several generations of inbreeding. So we were forced to try and find other reindeer and see if we could get them to fly with blood transfusions from our surviving 'flying' deer. They could indeed fly, but they became addicted to the blood. Soon they became wild and killed my remaining deer like some kind of zombie. Craving more blood, they escaped from my idiotic elves and the rest is history."

Steve continued to fly north. "So if that's true, what happens now?"

"I need a new mode of transportation. Do you love flying, Steve?"

"I do, in fact."

"How would you like to fly everywhere in the world in just one night?"

"Um, is that even possible?"

"You let me worry about that," Kris gruffed.

"I thought Santa was jolly."

"I only gotta put on that facade one night a year, thank God."

"Excuse me." Nisha had spoken for the first time in half a day. "You said you needed eight reindeer, right?"

Kris nodded.

"So when we met you, we counted five. Then there was the one stuck in the cave and the one you shot on the hill. That's only seven."

"Well, I'll be…" Kris said.

Suddenly the plane shook violently and there was a loud snapping sound.  Steve glanced out the window in a panic to watch something attacking one of the wings of the plane. The wing flew off to disappear amongst the clouds.

The plane began to spiral down into the darkness.

# HOME FOR THE ZOMBI-DAYS

A. P. FUCHS

There was no other tree like it.

Roy Davies swore up and down it had been reserved just for him. Or, at least, a guy like him full of Christmas cheer, blood pumping with hot cocoa, images of his family and their smiles dancing in his head.

Ol' Sammy Dean said he had something special for him when Roy called in to Sam's Treetop Top Trees Christmas Lot early that morning. The plan was to get a jump on all the other tree-buyers by hitting the place early, even wait outside the fence a few minutes before the lot opened with anyone else who was crazy enough to get there at seven in the morning, and forfeit a Saturday's sleep-in.

Except Roy didn't count on Old Man Winter sending a dilly of a blizzard, covering the town of Dellisburg with two feet of snow. The white stuff came down in sheets for most of the morning, but the sky had cleared by early afternoon.

Roy's truck wouldn't budge out of the driveway, so he spent an hour shoveling to clear it up. Sure, after that the truck moved, but it only reached the bottom of the driveway before hitting a snow ridge that it couldn't clear.

Roy had no choice but to wait.

The afternoon wore on. He sat on a fold-out chair on the landing of his house, looking out the window of his screen door, waiting on the town to send a few street plows through.

The first showed up around two.

Roy got in the truck and headed out to Sammy's lot, hoping to snag a tree before anyone else did, wanting to get it home in time for when his wife and kids returned from visiting his mother-in-law in Alberta. He just hoped the storm had been localized and they would still make it through on schedule, getting home just after midnight tonight.

It was slow-going getting to Sammy's. Most of the time Roy was stuck behind a plow, waiting for the big bulk of a machine to clear the road before he could even drive on it. But it didn't matter. The wait was worth it and he had plenty of time.

He checked the rearview mirror. No one was behind him. Either no one else was coming out to claim a tree or they were taking an alternate route. According to his GPS, he was taking the fastest way.

*Suckers*, Roy thought. *See you at the finish line.*

Twenty-five minutes later, the street plow turned off at the yield. Roy continued in a straight line, the road still covered in snow but packed down. It looked like dozens of other cars had already been up this way, having come in from the south.

Mr. GPS had lied. At least, in terms of time. It was still the fastest route but the snow plow slowed Roy down a whole lot.

"No matter," he muttered. "Another ten minutes and I'm there."

He drove on.

Only a few minutes in and the sky went gray. A few minutes more and the snow came down. Another minute and there was nothing but white in front of the windshield.

Roy had to pull over almost immediately the snow was so bad. He tried his cell to call ahead to Sammy's and say he was still coming.

No signal.

So he waited, running the heater intermittently, hoping the snow would die down soon.

It didn't. Roy got out of his truck and hit the road with his toes frozen. So were his fingers. His nose, well, he'd lost feeling on that hundreds of meters back; same with the tips of his ears. He was never one to dress for the snow. Car heaters, he figured, had a job to do and he was more than glad to let them do it. Besides, he hated all those layers anyway. Now he regretted not listening to his wife's naggings about dressing for the weather and even wearing an extra layer "just in case," especially since his heater had conked out on him as if it knew he was counting on it to stay warm in this stupid blizzard.

Sam's Treetop Top Trees Christmas Lot had to be up there just ahead, somewhere behind the veil of white that made it near impossible to see more than five feet in front of him.

He just hoped he would get there in time and get warm before he became a Roy-sicle forever.

* * *

They say that mirages only happen in deserts. Something about the heat draining all the moisture from your body, even drying up your brain so you start seeing things that aren't there. No one ever said you started seeing things in the cold, namely a blizzard where there was only white, white and more white.

There was a shadow up ahead, looking something like a fuzzy rectangle with a spotted triangle made from mozzarella. There were other triangles as well, fluffy and somewhat transparent behind the snow.

Roy, forehead frozen, pressed on against the cold wind, hoping to God he would make it to…to... He didn't know where he was supposed to make it to.

Tree Samtop Christmaslot Tree Stop or something.

Fuzzy, fluffy mozzarella. Fuzzy, fluffy toes; numb and fat. Fingers that were probably very well blue.

153

Treestop Samlot StopChristmas Tree.

Roy blinked—then couldn't open his eyes. The bits of frost from the wind caused tears to freeze his lashes shut. He squeezed his eyes together, hoping the skin-on-skin from doing so would be enough to melt the ice so he could see again. It helped, but only a little.

Stoplot Tree ChristmasTop Trees.

Too cold.

So cold.

* * *

A sharp rod of pain spiked through Roy's heels, drove right through his shin bones and slammed into his knees. His thighs ached just above the kneecaps as warmth blasted through his system.

"Yaaaahh!" he shouted.

"Hold it steady, mate," an old, pebbly voice said.

"No, no fries for me, thanks," Roy said. A flashback to the mozzarella: "Two slices for a buck? Okay, but hold the chocolate."

"Love to, friend, but I don't think you're thinkin' straight. No, surely not."

Roy's head went warm, then fuzzy, then warm again.

His legs pounded from the knees down. There was no way he was walking.

The old voice again: "Hurts, I know, but you'll thank me later. This here ain't just hot water. I did that I'd probably ensure you'd lose a toe or something. Maybe more. What you got here is what I call 'The Blend.' At least, that's the name I'm thinking of giving it. Never made it before, but have thought of it for years. Call me crazy, but warm water and some of the sap from my trees will make you just fine and dandy. Sap's supposed to have magical properties, so say some legends I heard. I don't buy it, but it sure is fun thinkin' it."

Roy groaned.

The old voice went on. "Maybe I should call it 'Sam's Warmer Upper Before Supper'?" He let off a whooping chuckle then followed it off with an old-timer's cough. "Nah. 'The Blend' works just fine for me. Listen, you're blue in the legs, my friend. This stuff'll help. Sap's supposed to be good for all sorts of things. You know, kind of like honey—syrup stuff—and killin' colds is one of honey's big things. So Mama used to say back in the day."

"I don't…" Roy started but the words slipped off his tongue, and a moment later he forgot what he was trying to say.

"Anyway," ol' Sam said, "I know you came for the trees. Saw you hobbling up the road. Saw you fall. 'No good weather to be out in,' I said. So I come and got you. Still blowin' up a snow cone out there. We're gonna have to just wait 'er out 'til she's done. Then I'll take you home. Know where you live?"

"Manersh sha blin errr…" Roy said.

"No matter. I'm sure you got a wallet on you somewhere."

* * *

Roy's world was black. The fresh scent of pine and burnt wood hit his nostrils. Despite wanting to open his eyes, he couldn't. The smell from the pine and wood filled his nose, went down his throat and hit his lungs. He tried moving, but the best he could do was wiggle his toes. They were in something liquid, something warm and something sticky.

A craggily voice hung over his head like a wet blanket, each sound it made just that: sound without meaning.

Head hurting, confusion setting in, the sound of his heartbeat began to fill his ears and pulse away, each *thump-thump, thump-*

*thump* getting louder as if it was pumping inside his head instead of in his chest.

Muscles aching, he tried to move again, but like before the most he could manage was wiggling his toes. The sticky liquid sloshed over his feet, its warmth sending goosebumps up and down his skin.

There was a hot tingle, then extreme relaxation as he felt every muscle in his body turn to quivering jelly.

His heart pounded, the beats growing slower apart.

Roy thought he was shaking, but couldn't be sure. That voice sounded overhead and still held no meaning.

The beats slowed even more, and the inside of his chest began to feel hollow, as if something inside was slipping away.

The sticky fluid splashed up and hit his legs. He realized he was indeed shaking.

*Thump.*

*Thump.*

*Th—*

* * *

The sweetness of the pine's sap rested on Roy's tongue, every inch of skin inside his mouth coated with the sticky stuff.

When he opened his eyes, a man's face was before him, the fellow with his hands on either side of Roy's head.

"You there, mate? Your color's gone. All pallid, you are. The Blend was supposed to warm you, not freeze you out again."

"Hrrrmm…" The sound trickled out of Roy's mouth.

"That's it. Wake up. Let's get you out of…" The man glanced down at Roy's feet. "The bucket's empty. Where's the Blend? It's as if you sucked it right up through your feet and…"

Roy put his hands on the man's arms and held them there. The fella's old face looked familiar, but no name came to mind. Roy licked his lips, the sweetness of the sap gone.

Where was it? What was he drinking that was so good, so sweet? It had to be around here, had to be…

The texture of the man's skin beneath his palms, tender, appealing. He smelled good, too, the scent stirring his stomach, making it rumble. Slowly, Roy brought the man's hand off one of his cheeks and dragged it across his skin to his mouth. The man's hands smelled of the delicious sweet stuff. Roy stuck out his tongue and licked the inside of the man's palm.

"Now, hey, there just a second. You can't…" The moment the man pulled his hand away, Roy jerked it back. He couldn't help himself and bit into it. Warm blood spurt into his mouth. The man howled and ripped his hand away, cradling it against his chest like a baby.

Roy stood, whatever that red stuff was that came out of the man's hand was even sweeter than the sap of a pine. He had to have more. Had to have that delicious sweetness on his tongue all the time. Legs heavy, head tipped to one side no matter how hard he tried to straighten it, Roy slowly moved toward the old man.

Tears in his eyes, the man said, "Roy, it's me Sam. What're you doing? What's happened? Why are you…"

Sam took a step back. Roy forced his legs to move faster. He raised his arms and reached forward. The old man looked like he was going to turn away from him, so Roy fell forward, his hands landing on Sam's shoulders. Roy's weight was enough to set the old guy off balance and pull him to the floor.

"Mrrrr…" *More.*

He let his head flop onto Sam's and he started biting into the old man's face. His teeth tore away the flesh from the cheeks despite Sam's open mouth screaming in pain. If anything, Sam's screams made it easier, because it stretched the skin and made a larger surface area for him to bite into.

Roy slurped the slab of chewy skin into his mouth, relishing the sweet flavor of the blood upon it. The two combined made him go into a frenzy. He grabbed Sam's head, torqued it to the side, and inadvertently snapped the old man's neck.

Roy ripped into the geezer's throat and tore out his trachea, crunching down on it like corn on the cob. Every mouthful made him want more and he ripped away Sam's clothes and dug into the old man's abdomen like a dog burying a bone. Intestines boiled over the rim of the bloody cavity like noodles and sauce over a pot. Roy gorged on them, their slick texture sliding down his throat like raw squid.

With each mouthful, he wanted more. He dipped his hand into the old man's body and pulled out the liver and bit down on it like it was pizza.

Growling, he chomped it down and knew that once the flesh from this man was gone, he would want more. But where?

He'd find something. He had to.

When he was finished, Roy got up, letting chunks of meat and strings of bloody skin roll off his mouth and chin and down his body. Eyes fixed forward, he stumbled to the door and left. While outside, something pulled him to the right. He didn't know where he was going, but moving this way seemed the right thing to do. The partly-covered tracks in the snow said someone else had been this way before.

He walked on.

* * *

"Roy?" Elena called from the front door. "Roy, we're home!" She looked down at Stephanie, their daughter. "Why don't you take your boots off and find Daddy?"

"Okay."

For a six-year-old, Steph was already adept at putting on and taking off her ski pants and parka, but still needed help with the wrap-around-the-head scarf thing though.

Before Steph left the foyer, she asked, "Should I tell him about Grandma and Grandpa coming over, too?"

Elena smiled. "Let it be a surprise."

Steph grinned, mimed zipping her lips shut, locking them, and throwing away the key. Elena gave her a wink. The little girl ran off into the house.

Elena hoisted the two duffel bags from their trip over her shoulders and climbed the stairs to the master bedroom so they would be ready for unpacking later. As much as she wanted to see her husband right away and plant a big, wet kiss on his face, it was more important to her that their daughter spent a few minutes alone with him first because she had been so excited to see him. It was all she'd talked about on the trip home.

Elena dropped the bags on the bed then made her way back down the stairs. When almost at the bottom, a high-pitched shriek shook her to the core.

"Steph!" she screamed, then jumped down the last step and headed for the kitchen. "Where are you?"

The girl screamed again.

Downstairs!

Elena ran down the stairs to the family room. Her foot caught on a step about halfway down and folded under her. She was on her butt instantly and slid down the stairs. She hit the bottom in a heap.

The screaming turned to a wet gurgle.

Then nothing.

The family room was empty, just the sofa, the loveseat and the big, microfiber chair that she and her husband fought to sit on all the time. The flat screen TV was there, turned off.

There was no…

The laundry room!

Her foot hurting something fierce, she forced herself up and limped to where the small room ran off the TV area, just beside the bar. The light was off, the door slightly open.

*Call the cops*, she thought. *Steph!* She had to know her daughter was okay.

She slowly neared the door and debated saying hello.

*Stay quiet. Just see who's there first.*

Elena crept up to the small opening and listened.

A soft sound came from the dark room: wet and slurpy.

She pushed on the door; it opened with a whiny creak.

The slurping stopped and a pair of drooping, white eyes gazed up at her from the dark.

"Roy!" she said and flicked on the light. "Roy?"

Her husband sat on the floor, their daughter in his lap, chunks of Steph's face dangling from his lips. Blood dribbled off his chin, the droplets splashing against the open flesh of what was once Stephanie's cheekbone. Their daughter gazed up at the ceiling, eyes open, never blinking.

Screaming, Elena turned and ran. *Grab her! Get Steph out of here!* But her legs refused to turn her around. She tumbled over a few steps later, her bad foot giving out from under her.

"No, no, no…"

Roy appeared in the doorway and hobbled toward her, dragging Stephanie's limp body by the foot behind him. Her husband's skin was blue and bruised in nasty blotches that covered his face and neck. He still had on his jacket and boots. His hands were blue as well, with dark sores on his fingers. Blood coated his face, chunks of moist flesh dotting his cheeks and forehead, as if he had stuffed his face into a bag of hamburger like a dog did to a snow bank.

Elena crawled along the ground, trying desperately to get her legs underneath her.

When she finally managed to get up and get most of her weight on her good leg, Roy grabbed her from behind. She swung around and backhanded him, but not before he tried to snap the hand off with his mouth. Fortunately, he didn't.

Breaking loose, Elena quickly limped to the stairs and, with tears in her eyes, began the brave ascent to higher ground.

As she hobbled up the stairs, the *thump-slap* of Roy's footfalls pulsed behind her.

"Come on," she said through gritted teeth, "move it!" A few more stairs and…she was at the top. She desperately wanted to catch her breath but a *thwoomp-bump* behind her caused her to glance over her shoulder. Roy had fallen face first on the stairs, his blue-gray hands with black fingernails clawing at the steps as he tried to regain his footing.

The front door. She had to reach the front door. Elena ran as fast as she could through the house. Her heart leapt in her chest when the front door came into view. Elated, she ran even harder for it, hand already reaching out for the knob. She quickly snapped it back when another blue-gray man appeared in front of her, his eyes dull, green mucus oozing from between his lips. The portly old-timer reached for her. She slapped his hand away and did a one-eighty, heading back down the hallway in the hopes of making it to the patio door off the kitchen.

The old man behind her groaned, his clumsy footfalls thumping the wooden floor in heavy *whumps* as he followed suit.

Roy reached for her with both hands the moment he was at the top of the stairs. Elena hugged herself as she twisted by, narrowly avoiding him. She entered the kitchen, slipped on the linoleum, and hit the floor face first. A dull, echoey spike of pain blasted through her nose and into her forehead and cheekbones. Tears suddenly springing from her eyes sent the kitchen into a blurry mosaic of brown rectangular shapes dotted with silver.

Low moans droned somewhere behind her.

Elena pushed herself onto her feet, her head immediately swooning as she stood. She stumbled back a step…and into a pair of waiting blue-gray hands behind her.

Screeching, she tugged herself away, but not before a burst of wet warmth gushed onto her shoulder, soaking into her shirt. The pain came after. Then there was no feeling in her right arm from shoulder to fingertips.

"Stop! STOP! *STOOOOOPPPPPPP!*" Elena shrieked as she made her way to the patio door. With each footfall, pain shot through her arm, the swinging motion only adding to the agony.

At the sliding patio door, she found the handle with her other hand and pulled. The door opened about a foot. Elena went to open it some more, but Roy slammed up against the glass right in front of her, his weight against the door making it impossible to open any further.

"Get away! Getawaygetawaygetaway!" she screamed, and instinctively lashed out at him with her left hand. Roy caught it and yanked her fingers to his mouth, ripping them free with his teeth. Blood spurted out of the stumps like geysers; throbbing pain shot up her arm and seemed to punch her in the face.

Dizzy, Elena swung herself sideways through the foot-wide opening in the door, doing everything she could to get herself outside and her hand away from Roy's mouth. The dead man held on, his grip solid, fighting her every effort. She pulled and pulled and…her arm dislocated in its socket. Pain shook her upper body and she fell out of the house and onto the patio.

Crawling along the deck, wriggling her hips and legs to move forward, eyes still blurry from tears, panic accelerating her heart with every moment, her first thought was how the deep snow didn't feel that cold at all. If anything, it felt as if it wasn't there.

White snow.

A series of sharp pricks hit the rear of her calves. A second later, red droplets rained down around her, dying the snow just in front of her a rich crimson.

Off in the corner of the yard was an old evergreen, one that she and Roy had planted back when they had first moved in. She loved its color. Always had. Its green matched the red on the snow.

Something heavy landed on top of her. Then something else.

She thought she heard Roy whisper something. Then again, it could have been her imagination.

"Merry Christmas," she thought she heard him say. "Glad you're home for the Holidays."

But it wasn't Roy's voice or the old man with him.

A little girl's head landed in front of Elena; Steph's wide eyes wrapped loosely around her skull was all that remained of her princess.

Elena couldn't feel her legs anymore. She still didn't feel the snow.

The evergreen looked on.

A bruised hand knocked some snow over her eyes.

Everything was blue-gray.

# FESTIVAL OF BONES

MICHELE ROGER

Christmas Eve morning was cold and damp, with a layer of fresh snow on the ground. Children of the city were gathering outside of the old Macy's department store window, between the Faygo soda stand and Detroit State Bank. They pointed at the classic toys; train sets and dolls, guitars and books, while teasing one another about what they might open from Santa the next morning. Their parents held steaming cups of coffee, while they chatted with one another, occasionally stopping to glance over at the podium. Detroit had become a city of less than ten thousand since the epidemic. Santa's visit took days to complete in other cities like New York and Chicago, but in Detroit, the whole Christmas gift selection took less than a few hours, leaving plenty of time for Christmas Eve dinner and celebrating.

The smallest kids gathered in the front of the crowd, happy to play and laugh with each other. Holiday school break had just started and the feeling of freedom rested solemnly on the teenagers gathered in small gangs. Two boys dared the others to go and touch the outer perimeter fence. A few boys, dressed in their hunting camouflage, hoisted gaunt looking girls up onto their shoulders to get a better look.

Martin McDonald joined them, his backpack filled with chopped-up squirrel parts and freshly-killed snowbirds. He passed out the bait bags to the other boys.

Several fathers stood talking about the new car contract in town and which of the Big Three might land it successfully, bringing in needed jobs and revenue for the city. They stood with their backs turned to the teenagers, acting like protective barriers between the bloody bags and their own small children. Mothers spoke of their clever, gaunt daughters and how proud they were of them. Several selected in other cities had been refused Santa's gift because they were too thin and sickly.

Christmas music played loudly over the speakers along the sidewalks. Mrs. Wilkins joined the mothers, hugging a few ladies she hadn't seen since her husband's funeral. Soon the people broke up into family groups as the time drew closer for the ceremony to start. Martin McDonald joined his father, rubbing his hands together in mischievous anticipation, while giving the other boys a big grin and a thumb's up.

Rachel, high atop Matthew Graves' shoulders, said she could see a cloud of snow, traveling low along the ground, heading their way from just beyond the green zone line. A ripple of silence rolled through the crowd. Heads turned and necks careened to get a better look beyond the fence. The large crowd followed her finger as she pointed at the cloud of swirling ice and snow. Mothers picked up their toddlers and held them close. Husbands put a comforting arm around their wives. Their attention was soon redirected as the Christmas music grew louder and a limousine pulled up behind the podium stage.

Mayor Brimm, dressed head to toe in a white fox fur coat, stepped out of the car and waved to his city residents. Security flanked him on either side as he walked along the icy sidewalk. The winter air blew like smoke from his perfect smile. It was a smile that widened as he saw the children wave back to him. *Ah, future voters,* he thought.

The mayor strolled up to the podium. The gait of his walk told his life story. Brimm was a gangster turned leader during the epidemic. He galloped up to the podium where a microphone was hastily adjusted. His assistant handed him a small tablet and he tapped the screen and began to read his speech, never once breaking his smile. "Merry Christmas to the best damned city in all the world! We are the city who never gives up. We are the city who put the world on wheels. Never, ever forget that, people! No matter the obstacle, we have persevered, be it beaten down by the man or beat up with disease, abandonment or a shit hand dealt at birth. The Lord will provide. We must remember to remain thankful for our lives and humble for what we've been given. Today marks the spirit of Detroit and holiday of good will, comfort and joy for every last damn creature tough enough to stay here. I ask you to bow your heads."

All gathered bowed their heads in reflection. The mayor, one part spiritual father, one part government leader, then broke through the silence once more. "Hey you kids, who's comin' to your house tonight?"

A handful of children yelled, "Santa!"

The mayor put his hand to his ear and leaned towards the small children in the front. "Who?"

The crowd answered in a roaring, mocking cheer, "Santa!"

"That's right," Mayor Brimm roared with enthusiasm. "I think I hear him coming down the street now!"

Directly on cue, a sleek, cherry red Mustang roared around the corner, punching the throttle up to ninety miles per hour and doing two laps around the heart of Campus Martius before squealing its tires and stopping in a cloud of smoking rubber next to the podium.

The mayor laughed slyly. "Who needs eight tiny reindeer when you got four hundred and twenty horses; you know what I'm sayin'?"

The mayor walked coolly over to the mustang and opened the passenger door. A fat man, dressed in a red coat, looking tired and weary, stepped out.

A few of the children yelled, "Santa!"

He shook the mayor's hand and the two men made their way to the podium.

The mayor took the mic again. "Thank you, Santa, for arriving today to help us in our ceremony. Thanks to our census, we've sent a text message to every damn person listed as head of household in the city. Parents and grandparents, please check your cell phones." Men and women of all ages held up their devices as their screens glowed brightly. "Santa will be helping me to determine who'll be chosen to receive the gift of the city." The mayor turned to Santa and asked him to randomly choose one phone number from the list in the mayoral tablet.

Santa looked out into the crowd. He couldn't help but see the somber faces of the teenagers and adults. He pushed his way past the mayor and said quietly, "It's my belief that every creature deserves the basic comforts that we as a human race can provide, especially at this time of year." His words were sincere but his expression was anguished as he scrolled through the tablet and finally hovered his mitten-covered fingers over a random phone number. Before he placed the call, he added, "I know that there are many myths about me and this gift giving. Whoever is chosen in the end will receive the gift no matter if they're half-starved or healthy, young or old. A gift is appreciated no matter who or what you are." A few of the mothers in the crowd gasped. Several girls wobbled on their pencil-thin frames, objecting, saying that they had read how they could be passed over on receiving the gift from the city if they were too thin and sickly, and not being found worthy. Their panic increased as the snow just outside the outer fence rolled and kicked in a cloud of activity. From the cloud came the faint sound of wailing and growling. Santa turned to see the inevitable approaching. He took a deep breath and touched the tablet. Anxiety-filled silence fell over the crowd as they listened for the ringing of one phone.

Mrs. Wilkins trembled as she placed the phone to her lips and answered, "Hello?"

Cueing the music over the speakers, the mayor shouted her name like a game show host selecting a contestant. "Mrs. Emma Wilkins, you and your family have been selected by Father Christmas himself! Come on up to the podium and introduce us to the rest of the Wilkins clan." The mayor was bursting with energy as his assistant hurried the woman and her family to the podium. Santa and the mayor clapped and the rest of the crowd followed their lead. A single grandmother and three adult children, two girls attending Wayne State, and a boy who worked a successful meat stand at the Eastern Market, held one another close as they timidly made their way towards Santa. Santa hugged each of them as they came on stage. When he was finished, he gave a wholesome, "Ho—Ho—Ho!" in a feeble attempt to lighten the mood.

The boy, not more than twenty, turned to the mayor and began to argue, "Our grandmother just lost her husband to cancer this spring. It isn't fair! Our family should be exempt from receiving the gift."

The mayor just kept on smiling. He smoothed out his fox fur lapel and continued with the ceremony, ignoring the boy's protests. "And now, we call for the gift of the city. Who do we have for this very important honor?" A small boy dressed as an elf came up to the stage and presented Santa with four golden orbs, each sitting perfectly on a red velvet pillow. The boy presented the pillow to Father Christmas as if he were presenting a crown to a king. Meanwhile, a motor kicked on and a large extension of the small staircase at the back of the stage slowly extended outward towards the outer fence and beyond its secure edge.

By this time, the snow cloud had settled and the residents of Detroit could see their former neighbors. Not quite dead but not quite living, the zombies were the survivors of a brutal epidemic that had killed off over half of Detroit's population. The little elf boy began to count them. He looked up at the mayor and said, "There's a lot more of them this year, sir."

The mayor put his hand cautiously over the mic to prevent the crowd from hearing.

Santa turned to the Wilkins family, "You know they'll all freeze to death if they don't have living flesh and blood to consume. It's our duty as a human race to help the sick and homeless. One of you will be selected to be the gift of this city, to keep our less fortunate neighbors alive until such time that a cure is discovered. God bless you for your act of giving."

Martin McDonald broke free from his parents with a few of the other boys. They ran to the fence and threw their bloody chum bags into the throng of zombies. The bags broke open just under the fully extended platform. A few girls screamed as the zombies began to fight over the chopped, bloody scraps, ripping and tearing at one another for the tiny bit of food.

The mayor turned his back to the crowd. From his front pocket, he presented the handle of a small .38 caliber gun.

Santa sighed at the unnecessary tactic. He whispered to both the mayor and the sobbing Wilkins women, "I find your use of weapons highly condemnable, Mayor. I'm sure that this fine woman would want her neighbors to be fed and cared for if it were one of her own children out there beyond the fence."

Santa directed Mrs. Wilkins and her children out along the platform gently. Once the family was on the extended cat walk, the mayor returned to the safety of the podium. Santa joined the Wilkins as they trembled. He offered each of the girls and Mrs. Wilkins a golden orb tied with a shining ribbon. The boy was given the remaining orb by default.

Some of the healthier zombies below the Wilkins family jumped and grabbed at their feet. The more desperate ones fought and rolled in the snow, fighting for the scraps of feather and bone from the bait the boys had thrown. They were working themselves into a frenzy, and the families pressed closer to the fence to get a better look.

The mayor began shouting over the mic, making Mrs. Wilkins cry. "Back up, people! You know better than to get near that electrified fence!" He pulled the mic away but his voice trailed off as he cursed and directed Santa, "Goddamn it! Let's get this over with. I'm about to have a lawsuit on my hands over some brat who gets cooked from being pressed against that damn fence by gawkers."

Santa closed his eyes and listened to the snarls and screeches below the catwalk. He took a deep breath and said, "Merry Christmas! Please open your gifts." One at a time, the Wilkins family opened the golden orbs. Mrs. Wilkins was first, then each of the girls opened their orbs to find a tiny, gold-gilded bone. They each looked at the sadistic charm with confusion and repulsion.

The mayor smiled and raised his hands to the crowd and everyone applauded. When the boy opened his orb, a bloody chicken bone popped out and tumbled onto the platform. Immediately, the boy began to scream, "No! We should be exempt. I'm the only man of the house left! Exemption! Exemption, please!"

Pulling the women quickly towards him, the mayor separated the Wilkins family in a blur of activity. Dragging the sobbing women to the podium, the mayor held them tightly in his arms and countered, "My administration has always believed in equal rights for men and women. No family requires a male head of household. Don't you agree?"

With the crowd distracted for a brief second, Santa took his cue and pushed hard on the lever attached to the platform extension. The extension gave way, its end falling violently into the snow, scattering the zombies. Jacob Wilkins went tumbling down the catwalk and into the center of a mad feeding frenzy.

The undead survivors of the epidemic tore his shirt as if it were wrapping paper. They yanked off his belt as if it were ribbon. They tore at his face and feasted on his blood.

A few lucky ones ran off with huge chunks of flesh, an intact arm or a whole knee joint.

The weaker ones gnawed on his bones until all that remained was part of his shoe, a button from his pea coat and a small golden orb, which glistened in the bloody snow.

# KILLING CHRISTMAS

## IKTOMI

"We're going to kill Christmas," Jody said.

I looked over at him and rolled my eyes. "And how are we going to do this?" I asked.

"It's simple, Belle, baby, we get the right ingredients for the spell and we'll take the whole motherfucking thing down."

I shook my head. Jody always went on about spells and magick ("Always spell it with a 'k' at the end" he would say) and how he'd sold his soul to a demon two years before we met. I didn't believe a word of it, of course, because Jody was always a little weird, and starved for attention.

Who could blame him? He was a scrawny guy who was pale year round, even during our hot summers. If he went out into the sun he would get burned, and unlike any other normal person, his burn didn't turn into a tan. It flared red and painful until one day it was white again. He had long black hair and loved metal music, which I guess you could figure out with the spells and devils and all of that.

But it was more than just some kind of adolescent trip with Jody; he meant it. This was part of what had attracted me to him. I was a decent-looking girl with a nice figure and plenty of friends, and if I really wanted to date or be more popular than I already was, I had a lot of options. My Dad had money, too; real money, so there was that. But not one of my friends was as real as Jody. Not one. They were all full of shit.

While most people thought Jody was the one truly full of shit—and to be honest, I thought the same many times—he had the heart of someone who was real. He tried, man, he really tried, to be a different, real, stand-up person. For him that meant Satan and Cookie-Monster vocals, and that was okay by me. I dug the music, too.

But that day, the afternoon of the twenty-fourth of December, when he told me he was going to kill Christmas, was the day where everything changed, when my admiration for his rebellion changed to one of horror and fear. Because here's the thing:

Jody really did kill Christmas.

*   *   *

He gathered all the materials he needed. I'm not sure how he got the ingredients, because a lot of them were pretty weird and hard to find, but he did. The afternoon of the twenty-fourth he mixed them up in what he affectionately called his 'cauldron.' It was a giant iron pot he'd found in the woods behind my house two years before. Apparently, some homeless family was living out there and they were using the pot to cook food in. They'd moved on, but the pot had stayed, and Jody found it. He consecrated it to Satan a year later and ever since then, it's been sitting in the basement of his parents' house, collecting spiders. Not now though. He broke it out and set it up on some iron slates he'd found. He piled some wood underneath it, and after cleaning it, he burned the wood, letting it cleanse the remainder of the pot. Then he opened a window so the smoke would roll out, but strangely enough, there wasn't much smoke at all; just a tiny wisp.

I watched him as he did this. He spoke some words in Latin, reversing them for full effect, and occasionally spat into the cauldron. It would hiss on impact and a tiny green flame would erupt for a brief moment before dissipating.

"I need your urine," he said.

"What?" I asked.

"Part of the spell calls for the bodily fluid of a non-believer," he explained. "I didn't figure you wanted to bleed into it, so pissing was the next best thing."

I was a little hurt that he'd called me a non-believer, although he was right. I guess my face must have shown what I was thinking.

"Look, Belle, it's okay you don't believe. It doesn't hurt my feelings any. Besides, I know how all of this sounds, but fuck it, I've seen the truth, baby. I've seen it and it's big and nasty and ugly. There's a god, all right, a god that couldn't give a shit about you or me if we gave our lives for Him. Just look how He treated His supposed son. And if there is a god, there's a Devil, and the Devil is where it's at. I sold my soul two years ago and these have been the best two years of my life. The best. I met you, we became friends, and all those fuckers that used to pick on me have all faded to the background. My mom doesn't bother me anymore and her asshole boyfriend doesn't come around much either. Good times." He stopped for a moment to catch his breath. "All I'm saying is, give me a chance to prove myself to you. This is it. If this spell doesn't work, I won't bother you about this Satan shit anymore."

I folded my arms across my chest. "We both know that's not true."

He laughed. "Come on. Please?"

I didn't think about it long. "Okay, get me a glass or something."

"No, no. Your fluids can't be fouled by touching another object. They have to be pure."

"Are you telling me I have to piss straight into the pot?"

He nodded and his face turned a little red. "Sorry, Belle."

I sighed. "Then you have to turn around. No peeking."

"Aw. Just a little look?"

"I'm going home."

"Okay, okay, I won't look." He left for a moment and came back with a ladder. He set it up next to the cauldron. "You climb up it part-way, pull down your pants, stick out your ass, and let fly," he said.

"All right." I did as he said, and even though it was awkward, it was doable. The thing was, I got nervous and I had a hard time letting it go. "Maybe you should leave the room, Jody."

"No way. I have to be here to add the next ingredient immediately."

"I can't go."

"Think about a dripping faucet."

"Shut up."

"Or what about a waterfall? Or think about the weight of the ocean. Man, all that water must be heavy."

Just like that, it happened. Urine gushed and I was afraid I was going to splatter myself. I closed my eyes and let it flow. I was just finishing up when he said, "So. You've got bush, huh?"

My face turned a deep crimson. "Asshole." I yanked my pants up. He was standing to the side, staring and smiling.

"Belle , that was awesome," he said.

"Well, maybe next time I'll pee on you. What do you think about that?"

"As long as I can open my mouth," he said with a smirk. He broke his gaze from me and turned back to his bag of goodies. He pulled out a sack of little pieces of bread and held it up for me to see. His eyebrows wiggled. "Consecrated host," he explained. He opened the bag and poured the contents inside. I imagined the spongy bread soaking up my urine and my stomach turned.

"Okay." He put his hands on his hips and sighed. "One last thing, Belle." He looked at me, his gaze hard and steady. "You have to promise me you won't run away when you see this."

"No way, Jody. I don't know what you're gonna do. I can't make that promise."

He grimaced. He seemed to think it over for a minute. "Fine, I've already come this far." He walked over to the corner of the room to the work closet where his family kept the mops, brooms and other cleaning supplies. He stalled for a moment by the door, glanced back at me, shrugged, then opened the door. Seconds later, he emerged with a garbage bag that held something round in it, something about the size of a basketball. He walked back over to the cauldron very carefully.

"What is it?" I asked.

"The severed head of a sinner," he replied.

I laughed. He didn't. He opened the bag and a bad smell wafted from it. When I say 'bad,' I mean 'bad' in the sense of, 'This meat has spoiled,' not, 'That's so cool.' He reached inside, balled his fist, and pulled out the head of Randy Carver by the hair.

I said nothing. I stared, fascinated and repulsed. I couldn't believe it. At first I thought it was all a joke but then I realized how wrong I was. That head wasn't fake. It was real.

"The spell called for the severed head of a sinner, and I didn't figure we'd find somebody as bad as Randy anywhere," he said. He held the skull over the cauldron.

Randy's brown eyes were open and dull. They looked like doll eyes. I'd seen him in school just two days ago, and those eyes had been alive and vibrant, if not filled with more than a little mischief. Now they saw nothing. His lips were closed, pursed together, as if in mid-kiss. Those same lips had been creased with laughter at me the other day. It was right after he'd slapped my ass when I walked by him.

"You know you like it, slut," he'd said.

That mouth wasn't moving now and it certainly was never going to speak again. The lips were too blue.

"I can't believe this."

"Believe it," Jody said. "I had to trick him into meeting me in the woods behind my house. I told him I had some drugs I could sell him and of course the asshole bit. I snuck right up behind him and knocked him out with a baseball bat." He turned the head around so I could see the back of it. "I put a big-ass dent in his skull. See?"

I saw it. I finally couldn't take anymore and I ran to the corner of the room and puked. I watched the chicken and rice I had for lunch splatter in the corner, hot and greasy, half-digested. Behind me, I heard Jody invoking the Lord Satan.

He ran through a litany of words. Some were in English, some in Latin, most in French. He rattled them off like he'd spent his entire life memorizing them, an actor ready for his big moment on stage, who was finally getting to play the role he'd always dreamed of.

I sat down next to my puke. I felt nothing other than a sour rumbling in my stomach. I watched Jody as he chanted but nothing registered. I'd gone numb. All the rest, all the cats he'd killed and the blood he'd taken from his own body, all the rituals and stupid shit before today were all meaningless. It was harmless fun—unless you were one of the cats. But this was all real. This was murder. There was no going back from it.

I decided to play along until I could leave. Then I would go tell the police. I had to. Otherwise, I was an accomplice.

Jody barked the name of Satan in some obscure Babylonian tongue I'd heard him use before, then he tossed Randy's head into the cauldron. He stepped back, smiling, waiting.

Nothing happened.

There was no burst of energy, no explosion, no gnarly tentacles, no phantasmal ectoplasm. There was just the cauldron, Jody and me.

He looked puzzled at first, then he grew angry. His face turned red and he kicked the side of the cauldron so hard that it tipped over and spilled its contents across the floor.

"You promised me!" he yelled. He looked at the floor, as if he were looking into Hell itself. "You promised me!"

Silence filled the room. The combination of my urine and the wine and host and the other ingredients pooled in the corner farthest from me, gathering around Randy's head, which was laying on its side. I stared at the mess, fascinated. I couldn't tear my gaze away.

Jody kept ranting and raving. He called Satan every name in the book and made up a few more. He stomped the floor and punched the wall a couple of times. He was so caught up in his anger that he didn't see what happened next. But I did.

Randy's eyes…blinked.

I gasped. Did I really see what I thought I saw?

They blinked again. They shifted in their sockets, scanning the room, checking everything out. Then their dull color flamed to life. I wouldn't say they were red exactly but they were a burnished crimson. His eyes settled on Jody and stayed there.

"Hey," Randy said. His voice was raspy and hard to hear over Jody's ranting. "Hey!" he yelled again.

This stopped Jody in his tracks. He stared at Randy's head like he couldn't believe it.

"Pick me up, kid," Randy said, although it wasn't Randy's voice. It was gruff and ancient, with a dying wheeze that made me think of old people tucked away in nursing homes.

Jody walked over, hypnotized. My stomach turned again. I had a bad feeling about this whole deal. I tried to say something but my mouth was dry. Only a rusty gasp came from me.

Jody picked up Randy's head and held it in front of his face.

"I got a secret for you, kid," the head said. "Put me to your ear. I don't want no one else to hear this."

Jody smiled and slid the head over next to his right ear.

Then he screamed. He threw the head across the room. It hit the far wall with a wet smack and fell to the floor. It rolled over so I could see its face. Randy was chewing a mouthful of Jody's ear, swallowing it down. Some of Jody's ear was stuck on Randy's chin.

Jody screeched and ran out of the room. He sprinted to the stairs and up them, calling out for his mother. It all would have been comical except now I was alone in the basement with an undead, possessed head, sitting next to my own vomit.

Randy glanced at me. "You want to know a secret, sugar tits?" he asked.

I jumped to my feet and ran for the door. He was cackling the whole time. I was almost out of the room when a pair of hands shoved me down. I hit the stairs, banging my head. I looked up, stars exploding in my vision.

Looming over me was a body sticky with blood, missing its head. Randy's body.

Its fingers clawed the air between us as the headless body bent down to grab me again. This time, though, I was ready. I kicked it in the chest and sent the body staggering backwards. It hit the wall and bounced off, its feet tangling. It fell to the floor but didn't stop trying. It kept crawling toward me, eager to get its hands on me.

I watched it for a tiny second, fascinated and repulsed by the sight.

"Hey! Come back here!" Randy shouted. It was enough to break the spell. I bounded up the stairs and into the kitchen. It was then I got my first inkling that everything was out of control.

Jody's mom lay on the floor, convulsing. Half her face was gone—and when I say gone, I mean gone. There was no flesh, no meat, no cheek bone, no teeth and no eye. There wasn't even the bone of the eye socket. It looked like someone had taken a shovel and scooped it all out and left her lying there.

Standing next to her was Jody. His hands were dripping with blood and he was eating his mom's face. He held half her jawbone in his fingers as he ate the pulpy flesh stuck to it like a starving man would eat a piece of cantaloupe. He licked between the teeth, making sure he got every little bit, slurping up the blood with his tongue.

Jody looked up at me. He smiled. Then he spoke, although it wasn't with Jody's voice. "Hey, bitch," he said. "Want some head?" He held the chunk of bone and meat out for me.

I screamed. I ran from the room and Jody laughed like Randy had laughed; a high, hard cackle, like a witch that just had her first orgasm. I was in the living room and headed for the front door when Jody's dad lurched into my path. His throat was slit end to end and blood poured from it, staining the front of his shirt. The slash marks were jagged and rough, like someone had used their teeth instead of a knife.

How did Jody get to them both so quickly? I had no answers. All I knew was to run. Jody's dad reached out for me, trying to grab me by my hair. I ducked under and threw an elbow into his ribs. I heard the bones crack. He staggered backwards and my fingers found the doorknob. I threw open the door and ran out into the fading light of day.

I crashed into a set of Christmas carolers who had just stepped onto the front porch, and were about to ring the doorbell. I sent them scattering, crashing to the ground. There was a fat kid with the group holding a fistful of candy canes, all opened and half-eaten. He was at the back, and when he fell, he jabbed three of the candy canes into his left eye. He screamed in agony.

I didn't pause. I was on my feet and sprinting towards my house, one block away. The sun was gone and it was night. How could that be? When we started the ritual, it had been close to two in the afternoon. Only a few minutes had gone by. It just wasn't possible.

The shrieks of the carolers broke me from my reverie. I slowed down enough to take a glance behind me. They were being attacked by Jody and his family. They were torn apart: stomachs ripped open, guts flung in every direction, fingers and toes eaten, skin ripped off.

One of the carolers pulled a pistol. Why someone out singing songs about the birth of the Lord would carry a gun, I had no idea. But he did. He slammed the muzzle into Jody's dad's mouth and pulled the trigger. Brains splattered the outside glass door of the house. Jody's dad sagged to the ground, defeated and unmoving.

It was just like the zombies I'd seen on TV only these weren't the regular kind, the ones that walked slow and moaned a lot. They were much quicker, almost like panthers. But here's the thing: they were spreading out.

The ones that Jody's family killed rose and attacked those still living.

I reached my home and ran inside, locking the door behind me. I was out of breath and sweating like a fat man chasing down a hot dog. The house was dark and empty; my folks had gone to visit the Hamptons across town. I was alone.

Outside, the screams grew louder. I heard windows shatter and glass break. A car hit its horn and screeched its tires. It ran straight into a house. I heard brick crack and tires pop.

The screaming never seemed to stop.

I went deep into my house, far away from any windows and doors. I knew it was only a matter of time before they came for me. Jody knew where I lived and he would arrive soon enough. There was nowhere to hide because by then I could hear them all through the neighborhood, the living dead, howling for blood and flesh. I heard others, too, out there shrieking, yelling, fighting for their lives.

Oh, what had Jody done? What had I done in helping him?

It wasn't me, I tried to tell myself. I was innocent. I was just there. I couldn't be blamed. Yet I'd let him go ahead with what he was doing, never giving a thought to stopping him. Did I really just think it was all a joke? Or had I secretly wanted the spell to work?

It was an absurd idea but there it was, and as much as I didn't want it to work after the fact, I had to admit to myself that part of me had been hoping it would work. I remembered thinking it would be nice to see proof of a world beyond our own. Now that I had the proof, I certainly wished I didn't.

I thought about the attic.

It was the safest place, I figured. The only way up there was by a pull-string ladder, and once I was there, no one could reach me. Maybe I could hide out until it all passed over, or until the authorities took matters into their own hands.

But it was too late for that.

The front door splintered with the sound of Armageddon. I ran from the hall to my bedroom. I wasn't sure what I was going to do, but I had to do something. Standing where I was meant certain death, and the attic was now too far away to consider.

In my closet I kept an aluminum baseball bat for protection, never really believing I'd ever have to use it. I snatched the bat up and ran back to the hall.

There was a zombie running towards me. It was Mr. Jeffers from across the street. He wore the same yellow sweater he did for weeks on end this time of year, only now it was stained with his blood. His tan Dockers had seen better days; grass marks slid up and down the legs. His face was relatively unhurt but his neck was opened wide. The gash yawned like an extra mouth. His eyes were blue except for that faint hint of crimson, just like I'd seen in Jody's.

He loped towards me, left shoulder down from where it had been somehow dislocated. Blood dripped from his mouth and off his chin; he was a scary sight to see.

"I finally got you, you bitch," he hissed.

I swung the bat with all I had.

The blow would have taken his head clean off, but he raised his arm at the last second, and instead of decapitating him, I broke his arm. The bone cracked like I'd hit a home run. His eyes turned a deeper, brighter red, and he charged me.

I ducked to the right and stuck out my foot, tripping him. He had no way to break his fall because one arm was dangling uselessly and the other was flopping from where I'd broken it. He crashed into my dresser, shattering his nose and front teeth. Mr. Jeffers screamed and rolled over but by then it was far too late for him.

I brought the bat down and destroyed what was left of his head. The aluminum clanked when it split his skull and his brains splattered out of his ears from the concussion. I raised the bat and slammed it down one more time, just to make sure. Before I left, I kicked him in the balls for good measure.

Down the hall, at the front door, I heard others entering the house. I ran for the attic string but it was too late. Four more zombies had flooded in just a few feet away from me. I didn't recognize most of them but figured they were other neighbors who'd been killed and transformed.

I turned and ran.

I slammed the door to my bedroom and pushed the dresser in front of it. This would only hold them for a few moments but that was okay; a few moments was all I needed.

The window to the backyard opened quick and easy and I punched out the screen with one good kick. I slipped down and out, landing on my feet. The air was cold and my teeth chattered almost instantly.

The entire neighborhood echoed with screams of agony and despair. I heard hundreds of voices raised in a cacophony that could only be matched by the denizens of Hell itself. In fact, it felt like Hell had been raised and deposited in my little town in Kansas. The sky roiled red, dark clouds spitting blue lightning and echoing with loud booms. No rain fell and I think that if it did, it would have been blood, because that exact moment froze like something I'd read about in the Bible, in the book of Revelations. I half-expected four riders to burst from the sky and bring judgment down on everyone. Zombies filled my open window behind me, their faces leering out at me, cursing, saying all sorts of foul and offensive things.

"Get the bitch!" one of them shouted.

I didn't stick around to wait for them to come. I bolted for the fence at the back of the yard, jumped over it, and fled into the woods. There was a mile-long and half-mile thick strip of woodland at the back of my neighborhood, and I felt my best chance at escape was through there. If I could get to the other side, I could reach Highway 64, and then surely flag down a passing car or truck and get a ride out of there. I had to alert the authorities, although I was pretty sure they'd already been alerted.

For the most part, my plan did work. I got through the woods with little trouble. The zombies stayed behind, killing and eating and converting as many into a demonic horde of walking death as they could, and there was nothing to stop them.

I got away, for a while. But the zombie disease spread like a wild plague, and before I'd gotten out of the state, three more towns became infected. The military moved in but there was no way they could do much now that it was all out of control.

Eventually, they nuked Kansas. Good riddance, I thought. That state was full of assholes anyway.

But of course that didn't work. Too many zombies had slipped past the quarantine zone and pretty soon any resistance was terminated. Wave after wave of them crashed along the shores of humanity and drowned the survivors with their weight in numbers and savagery.

Not all of us are dead. Some of us have survived. We made it to a small island in the Pacific. The living dead can't reach us unless they can swim, and so far, they haven't shown that kind of determination. Who knows, though? They'll probably build boats and come after us at some point.

Many think the plague was caused by the government, many others think it was some kind of virus that sprang up to thin the herd of humankind. But I know the truth. My friend Jody and I summoned something up from the bowels of Hell and it took possession of a corpse and made many others in its image. Are these other living dead simply unholy vessels for demonic spirits?

I think so. But in the end, it doesn't really matter how or why. Does it? I recorded these words for posterity, to admit my role in the disaster, in the culling of mankind. This is my confession. I've hidden it so it won't be found until long after my death. Only then can the world know.

The world has been lost; all because of one teenaged kid with an attitude problem, and one girl who was secretly in love with him.

# A VERY DEAD CHRISTMAS

## ANTHONY GIANGREGORIO

$W$elcome, dear reader, to a tale of Christmas, where things aren't always as they seem.

What do we mean? Read on and find out.

* * *

"$W$ell, everyone, this is the last of the reindeer meat," Mrs. Claus said as she sat the platter full of steaming meat on the center of the dinner table. "All the rest have become zombies." It was exactly one month until Christmas Day.

"Are you sure, Martha?" Santa Claus asked, his mouth already salivating at the aroma of the cooked meat. He was a fat bastard; there was no doubt about it. In the stories, he was described as round and jolly, but in reality, he was simply one fat mother-fucker. He had a glandular problem, and no matter how much he dieted, he just gained weight.

Not that this helped during the present food shortage that had hit the North Pole since the zombie apocalypse happened more than a year ago.

Martha sat down next to her husband, then let her eyes glance over the remaining elves sitting with them. "Yes, I'm afraid this is the last of our food."

There was Happy. "This sucks," Happy said, a perpetual frown on his lips. He was actually the absolute opposite of happy, which was where he got his name. It was supposed to be 'ironic.'

Next was Skinny. "Not to me, I love deer steak." He licked his lips at the sight of the still-sizzling meat. Skinny was almost as fat as Santa, only a few feet shorter. Once more, his name was supposed to be 'ironic.'

The next elf tried to grab a piece of steak but Martha slapped his hand with a ladle. "Not yet, Handsome Joe, we need to say Grace."

Of course, if you the reader are getting the whole theme here, Handsome Joe wasn't handsome at all. The best way to describe Handsome Joe was to take an asshole, stretch it so that it was the size of a face, then add some squinty eyes, a crooked nose, and a thin gash of a mouth. Handsome Joe was butt ugly, and that's not being 'ironic,' that was a fact.

The next elf was called Steve.

Yes, that's right: Steve.

What was wrong with him? What made his name Steve of all things?

How the fuck do I know? Steve is a good name, and that was what his mother named him. See? Fooled ya, didn't I? I bet you thought he was gonna have some kind of defect, like being a mutant or something. Well, the worst thing about Steve was that he was Republican, but we won't hold that over him—much.

"Hey, I heard that. I'm not Republican, I'm Libertarian."

Oh, sorry, about that Steve. Let's just say you're short and leave it at that.

"Fuck you, pal. I'm not short, I'm just not as tall as everyone else."

We're getting off track here, Steve, shut up and leave us alone. So, back to the story.

"Jerk," Steve muttered.

Oh yeah, and the rest of the elves names were Big Dick, Taint, Little Ripper, Mustache Ride and Smells Like Fish (or Fishy for short) and Slut, a female elf—you can try and figure out why Slut is named this on your own time. But here's a freebie. Slut loved to fuck.

"Are you going to say Grace this time, Santa?" Steve asked as he sat in his chair, waiting to eat. He was very well-mannered, and though his stomach grumbled, he had enough dignity to wait till it was time to eat.

"Grace?" Santa asked. "Fuck that shit. I'm fucking starving over here." He nodded to Martha. "Hey, babe, give me the biggest piece, and let's get down to eating. We can say Grace 'after' we've eaten." To emphasize his words, he leaned to the side and let out a mighty fart.

Being magic, the fart plumed out like a dark cloud and a face appeared. The cloud-face looked at each of the diners, winked once, then floated off to the ceiling, where it slowly dispersed.

"Well, that was a nice change of pace," Mrs. Claus said. "At least this fart was polite, not like some of the others." She glared at Santa, as if it was his fault when the farts would float from person to person, hovering around their face to let the person get a good whiff, and only then would it disperse.

"Hey, don't look at me," Santa defended. "My farts have a mind of their own. I don't control them once they leave my ass."

Martha sighed. "I declare, you're such a pig. Where the stories came from of you being fun, jolly, and sweet is a mystery."

Santa shoved a piece of deer steak into his mouth, then let out a loud burp. "I got a good publicist, babe. It's all in the image, you see, not what really is. Spread enough info around about someone and eventually some of it will stick like shit to a wall."

Martha sighed as she cut into her piece of steak. The elves were eating, too, and had been since Santa had farted.

Martha nibbled on her steak as she looked across the table at the others. This was all that was left of the North Pole residents. The rest of the elves had either died of starvation or had taken it upon themselves to venture out in search of help and supplies. Of course, the North Pole was isolated, so there was no help to be found. No doubt, those elves had frozen to death. She felt bad for them, but selfishly was glad they had left. At least that had made the remaining food stock last longer. It wasn't long before the reindeer were being slaughtered for their meat. Some had become zombies, but the ones that hadn't, had still suffered a fate as bad or worse than being zombified—they became food for the survivors.

Santa inhaled the rest of his steak, then he leaned over the table, and with a fork in each hand, snatched the remaining meat from each of the elves' dishes.

"Hey, what the fuck, Santa, I was eating that!" Happy snapped, angry that he'd lost his meal. The other elves looked the same but only Happy had the balls to actually say something.

Santa stood up, while still shoving the stolen meat into his mouth. He dropped the forks and spread his hands wide, challenging Happy. "What, Happy, you got something to fucking say to me? Come on, ya little shit, I'll squash you like a goddamn bug. You think you can take me on, bitch? Huh?" His eyes roamed over the others. "You think any of you can fucking take me? Then bring it on, motherfuckers! I'm the fucking boss around here, and don't you little pissants forget it." He let out another mighty fart and when it plumed up beside him, he directed it to go right at Happy and the other elves.

Santa turned and walked out of the room, grumbling about how this was 'His house,' and no one better try to take it from him. Martha gently placed her fork down and crossed her arms over her ample bosom. "I knew he could control them, no matter how much he denied it."

Happy was waving his hands around his head, trying to get the fart to dissipate, but the cloud just moved to the other elves, who sat still and took it. When the cloud finally rose to the ceiling and faded away, Steve pushed off from his chair and stood up. Of course, being so damn short, it still looked like was he sitting. But you get the point. He stood for dramatic effect, and though it didn't matter shit to the others, it made Steve feel good.

"We need to do something about that fat fuck." His eyes went right to Mrs. Claus. "Ma'am, I know he's your husband, but we can't keep going on like this. Maybe he won't hurt you, but the rest of us aren't as lucky. He'll kill us if he wants, and there will be no one to stop him from doing it."

Martha sighed wearily. "I know, Steve, but what do you want me to do? I still love the big jerk. He's just cranky because he's not getting enough to eat." She smiled at each of the elves. "You'll see, boys, once he gets some decent food in him, everything will go back to normal around here." She stood up. "Now, why don't you all go and attend to your chores. Someone needs to clean up the stable too; take care of all the blood from the last deer that was killed."

The elves, all grumbling to themselves, left the table, but Handsome Joe stopped and walked around the table to look up at Mrs. Claus. "You said that was the last of the food, is that right?"

She nodded down at him. She had become used to his butt-ugly face.

"So then, if there's no more food, what are we going to eat? What's Santa going to eat so that he'll calm down?"

Martha patted Handsome Joe's shoulder gently, like a mother to a son. "Don't you worry about that, dear. Precautions are being taken. Santa has a contingency plan in place for a situation like this."

"He does?"

"Yes, dear, he does. Now get going and go do your chores. At least if anything, it'll take your mind off of food for a while."

"Oh, okay, Ma'am, I guess you're right." He turned and walked away.

Martha watched him leave. She crossed her arms on the table and rested her head on her arms. Closing her eyes, she sighed yet again. She found herself doing that a lot lately. There was a lot to sigh about. No more food, Santa ready to explode, and the world having collapsed thanks to the dead walking. Things had never been as dire as they were right now.

* * *

Four days later.

All the elves shuffled into the dining room, hungry and exhausted. Due to the apocalypse, they were down to a fraction of the elf power they once had, and running the North Pole took a lot of hands.

There were the factories to keep going. Sure, the world might have been ruled by zombies, but toys still had to be made. Santa demanded it, and what Santa wanted, Santa got. He figured sooner or later the dead would be put down and then it would be business as usual, what with the gift giving, and the Ho-Ho-Ho shit he was known for.

As everyone sat down, only Santa and Mrs. Claus having not yet arrived, Handsome Joe looked around the table. He counted elves and came up one short. "Hey, guys, has anyone seen Skinny around?"

Steve looked over where Skinny would normally sit and he shrugged as he took in the empty chair. "No, I haven't. Come to think of it, I haven't seen him since yesterday." He leaned forward and made eye contact with some of the other elves. "Any of you guys seen Skinny around lately?"

Big Dick stopped talking to Little Ripper and glanced at Steve. "Who gives a shit about Skinny? The lazy, fat fuck is probably sleeping somewhere. Wherever he went, leave him be. More food for the rest of us."

"Yeah," Happy added. "The guy eats enough for three people; if he's not here, that's more for us."

Steve shrugged again, deciding he was going nowhere with the others. Handsome Joe frowned but said nothing. Maybe Skinny was sleeping somewhere, but one thing about the fat elf that everyone knew, the guy never missed a meal.

Santa came strolling into the room and sat down at the head of the table. He took one look at the talking elves and slammed his hand on the table, making the dishes and glasses jump an inch before coming back down to rattle for a second. "Enough talking! Shut the fuck up."

Most of the elves stopped talking but Handsome Joe was on a roll, and he kept going. When the others went silent, Handsome Joe's voice grew louder, and for the first few seconds, he didn't realize he was the only one talking, but he quickly figured it out when Santa roared, "Handsome Joe, how would you like a candy cane shoved up your ass? I said for everyone to shut up!"

Handsome Joe went silent and he looked down at the table. "Sorry, Santa, I wasn't paying attention."

Santa only growled in reply, mumbling something about butt-ugly elves. He shifted in his seat, as if he was daring someone else to speak. When he was satisfied he had control of the room, he leaned forward in his chair and slapped his hand on the table again. "Okay, so someone give me an update on how things are going around here."

"I'll do it," Steve said and stood up. He pulled a sheaf of papers from a hidden pocket and unrolled them, then began reading. "We're out of food, there's nothing to eat but ice and more ice. The factories are almost at a standstill due to not enough hands to work them. Communication with the outside world has gone completely silent; we haven't heard any kind of a transmission for over two weeks, and Skinny seems to have disappeared." He folded the papers and sat back down. Some of the elves began to mumble amongst themselves, but a glare from Santa silenced them once more.

"The factories need to keep running, Steve, you all know that," Santa explained. "We make toys here, and sooner or later we'll get back to normal, then those toys will be delivered. As for the food situation…" He managed a smile, which looked more like a grimace thanks to his overgrown white beard. "I procured some food for us. Martha is going to bring it in shortly, but until then, we need to make a plan for the future so that we're all still here when it comes."

Santa began laying out plans he'd come up with, how they needed to be strong and have hope that things would get better. A few elves asked some questions, but Santa mostly talked in circles, not really answering the questions, and sometimes actually twisting their questions back on them by asking a few of his own.

Steve was about to call Santa on his bullshit, no matter what the fat man's wrath might be, when Mrs. Claus entered the room, carrying a large, ceramic tureen filled with something brown. The aroma quickly filled the room, making all the elves and Santa salivate hungrily.

"Wow, Mrs. Claus, that smells fantastic," Handsome Joe said.

"I'm starving," Santa added, as the tureen was placed in the center of the table. All the elves tried to get a look inside the large bowl, but they were too short to see. Big Dick hopped up on his chair but a glare from Santa made him sit back down.

"Now, now, boys, there's enough for everyone," Mrs. Claus said with a smile.

"But we haven't eaten for days," Steve said, licking his lips with a rather dry tongue.

"Then give me your bowl so you can eat now," she replied and reached out for his bowl. Steve handed it to her, and a few seconds later, he had a steaming bowl of what resembled stew before him. Mrs. Claus quickly ladled out heaping bowls to the other elves, then Santa as well. Santa's bowl was double the size of the elves' dishes—not that they would have said anything.

Without waiting for anyone, Santa dug in, a lot of the stew getting in his beard. He ignored it, shoveling the food into his mouth hungrily.

The elves barely noticed, for they too, were eating with abandon. It had been days since they'd eaten solid food, as only water had been their diet, whether it was liquid or frozen, many of them chewing ice to stave off hunger.

Steve ate as well but not with as much gusto. As he chewed on a piece of unidentifiable meat, his spoon moved the stew around in his bowl. The meat was fatty, very fatty, and had a taste similar to pork. Now, where had Mrs. Claus found pork up at the North Pole?

"Say, Mrs. Claus," Steve said, "Where did you say you got this meat?"

"She got it at the 'shut the fuck up' store," Santa snapped. "If you don't want to eat it I'll be happy to eat yours." He reached for Steve's bowl but the elf slid it away from his gasp.

"No, Santa, I'm fine, I was just curious."

Santa licked his bowl clean, then held it out to his wife for another serving. "Good, because there's barely enough food to go around now, so if you don't want it, there's plenty who do. Isn't that right, boys?" he asked the other elves, who all replied in different ways, whether by nodding profusely or just voicing their agreement.

The rest of the meal was quiet, only the sounds of slurping and chewing filling the air. When all the stew was gone, Santa leaned back and rubbed his giant belly, burping once, then farting. The fart floated up and smiled to everyone, and with a wave floated away. Santa was content so didn't feel the need to send his fart at any of the elves. "Martha, baby, you did wonders with that meat. Outstanding, woman."

"Thank you, dear," she said and stood up and began gathering dishes. "Slut, will you give me a hand, please?"

The female elf did as asked, piling the bowls together and carrying them into the nearby kitchen.

"Okay, you assholes," Santa snapped. "You've all been fed, now back to work."

The elves began to file out, each smacking their lips and talking about how good the meal had been. The meat had been fatty, but it had still been delicious. Steve was the last to leave. He paused for a second, and asked, "I still don't understand where Mrs. Claus got the meat for that stew. You said all the reindeer are gone, and there are no other animals around us, and if that's so then…"

Santa rose to his full height and walked over to Steve; the word 'dwarfing' the small elf came to mind as the fat man towered over the short elf. "Steve, you've always been difficult. Now, do you mind telling me why when you were starving, and food was put before you, instead of being thankful, you have to question it all?"

"No, it's not that, Santa, it's just…"

"Exactly. Food has been provided, so just shut the fuck up and be grateful. Now get the fuck out of here and go back to work with the others." Santa cracked his knuckles, the gesture clear. *Get moving or get bitch-slapped.*

Slut popped her head out of the kitchen and she smiled at Steve. He was the only elf she hadn't fucked, and no matter how much she tried, Steve just wasn't interested. She figured he was gay. He wasn't, he just didn't want to stick his small dick where he knew everyone else had already been. Even Santa had taken a whack at that small snatch, or so the rumors around the Pole went.

With nothing else to do, Steve turned and left the dining room, his head shaking in frustration. He knew something was up, a mystery that needed to be solved, but with Santa hovering over him threateningly, he knew it was a mystery that would have to wait.

"Man, I gotta take a massive shit," Santa said to no one in particular. He picked up the North Pole Times and waddled off to the bathroom, a few farts popping out of his ass as he walked. They all floated away, not having any direction given to them by their master.

Steve went off to the factory to see how things were going.

*   *   *

Okay, let's keep this thing moving, we don't want you to get bored. So let's jump ahead a few weeks. Three and a half weeks to be specific. Like at the beginning of the story, everyone was gathered around the dinner table, only there was not as many people as when the story first began.

Steve was still there, and so was Slut, and so were Mrs. Claus and Santa, but the elf population had dwindled even more.

Big Dick was gone, and had been for weeks, and so was Little Ripper. Mustache Ride had disappeared a little over a week ago, and Taint and Smells Like Fish—or Fishy—to his friends, had been missing for two days.

Steve didn't like it at all. Worse, the stew was coming more regularly for dinner, but each time he tried to question Santa or Mrs. Claus on its origin, all he got was threats and changes of the subject.

In fact, Santa looked healthier than ever, and Steve was sure the fat fuck had put on some weight over the past few weeks. No, something stunk at the North Pole, and he was going to figure it out once and for all.

Maybe if Steve had been a little smarter he would have put two and two together by now. We're sure you, the reader, have figured out what's been happening.

"Hey, I heard that, you hack. I have figured it out, but I need proof before I can confront Santa with it," Steve snapped.

Oh really? Then what are you waiting for?

"Just you wait and see. I've got a plan." Steve did, too. When dinner was over, he gathered the remaining elves at the factory after closing and explained what he had in mind. He also explained his theory about Santa killing the elves and feeding them back to the remaining elves as dinner.

"Are you for real?" Happy asked, a large puss on his lips. "You think Santa has been killing us and Mrs. Claus is serving us up in her stew?"

"That's impossible," Slut added. "Mrs. Claus would never do that."

"I agree with Slut," Handsome Joe agreed. "She's too sweet to do something so horrible.

"Yeah, "Happy said. "Besides, if that was true, then that means we've been eating our friends." He blanched. "That's not something I want to think about."

"What don't you want to think about?" Steve asked. "That they tasted damn good, a lot like pork, or that they've been getting slaughtered one by one by the two people we once trusted."

"Neither," Handsome Joe said, frowning. "Ugh, I can still taste dinner. If what you say is true, then who did we just eat?"

"If I had to guess, I would say it was Fishy," Steve said.

Happy nodded, though he was looking sick. "Yeah, makes sense. The stew did taste a little fishy, come to think of it." He turned and vomited into a trashcan. "Oh, shit, I can't believe I just said that, or just ate that meal."

"But this might all be a big misunderstanding," Slut pleaded. "You might be wrong, Steve."

"That's why we need to get into Mrs. Claus kitchen and see what's going on. Haven't you noticed how no one is allowed in there alone?"

"But I help her wash the dishes all the time," Slut said.

"Yes, but that's after the meal, 'after' she's had a chance to clean up anything suspicious."

Slut considered that and it did make sense. Whenever she was helping Mrs. Claus, there had never been any of the meat lying out, and the large refrigerator was always locked. She hadn't given it much thought at the time, but now that Steve was calling attention to it, Mrs. Claus had been acting rather secretive. "Steve's right, guys, I don't want to believe it, but I think he's right."

Happy scowled. "So even if he is doing what you're saying, what the fuck are we supposed to do about it?"

Steve grinned rather evilly. "Simple. We get even."

* * *

So here we are again. To keep the story moving, let's just go to some cliff notes, all right?

Steve led the others into the kitchen, a crowbar in his hands. He broke the lock off the refrigerator and low and behold, can you guess what they found?

That's right. Elf bits. Mustache Ride's severed head was on the middle shelf in a pan, and a bucket of small intestines was on the bottom shelf. A pan on the top shelf held Big Dick's dick, and no one wanted to think about what 'that' was going to be used for. Smells Like Fish was present too, but the only thing truly there to identify him was the severed arm they found in the salad crisper.

See, there was a tattoo on it, one of a marlin on a hook. Fishy had gotten it years ago, on account of his name. He'd told everyone if he owned the name then it became his, and no one could use it to tease him. No one had really cared one way or the other, but the tattoo was still a hell of a way to know what part belonged to whom.

"That fucking fat bastard," Happy hissed as he stared at the contents of the fridge.

Slut backed away, a hand to her mouth in abject horror. She hadn't really believed what Steve had said, that is, not until this exact moment.

"So…w…what do we do now?" Handsome Joe asked as he sat on a chair and stared at the floor. He wanted to wash his eyes, scrub his mind of the images of his friends cut up like meat in a butcher shop.

Steve walked over to the butcher table across the room, the table now clean of blood. But Steve knew that only hours ago, one of his friends had been there, the small body lying on the table as Santa or Mrs. Claus had hacked and cut and sliced and diced the meat into bite-sized chunks for stew. There was a sharp cleaver on the table. Steve picked it up, holding it with both hands, as it was rather large for his small form. "We finish this," he snarled.

*　*　*

Santa had been dreaming of fucking supermodels when he was pulled from his slumber. His eyes snapped open, and he immediately knew something was terribly wrong. For one thing, he couldn't move his arms, and when he tried to move, he found that wasn't going to happen either.

"What the fu…" he began, but was silenced immediately by a slap to his chubby face.

"Shut up, Santa, you're not in charge anymore," Steve hissed.

Santa gazed up at the face of Steve in the gloom of his bedroom. Behind Steve stood Handsome Joe, Slut and Happy. For once, Happy actually looked 'happy.' Santa moved his head to the side to see that his wife was missing. "Where's Marth…" he began, but once more was cut off by a slap to the face.

"She's dead, fatso, and you'll be joining her soon enough," Steve said.

Santa's eyes went wide and it took less than a heartbeat for his look of confusion to turn into one of anger. "Why, you little fuck. Let me go right now and I promise to make yours and the others' deaths quick, instead of slowly like you all deserve."

Steve stepped a little to the right and Santa was able to see directly behind the small elf. He saw a large form on the floor, and it took only a moment for him to realize it was Mrs. Claus. She was dead, there was no doubt about it. There was a large candy cane sticking out of her right eye.

"That's to make sure she doesn't come back again," Steve said, answering Santa's unanswered question. "She tried to stop us; we had no choice."

Santa began struggling with his bonds again, but the elves had made sure he was good and secured. Santa wasn't going free unless the elves wanted him to.

But they had underestimated the fat man. He was lying on his side, his hands secured behind him, and as he and Steve talked, Santa let out the most raunchy, stinkiest fart he could force out of his large ass.

Like acid, the fart began to eat away at the rope securing Santa's hands, the foulness slowly corroding the twine that made up the rope. Santa could already feel the ropes loosening around his wrists, and his hands clenched into fists as he prepared to break free.

"What's the matter, asshole? Nothing to say now?" Steve asked through clenched teeth.

Slut ran over to the bed and got in front of Steve, her face only inches from Santa's. "How could you do that to the other elves? You made us 'eat' them for Christ's sake. Why? It's…it's inhuman."

Santa needed more time to let the ropes disintegrate from his wrists, so Slut's question was the perfect excuse to stall for time. Normally, he would never have bothered explaining himself, but now he did just that. "We were out of food, you all know that. I had no choice. It was either start eating the elves or starve to death once water wasn't enough to keep us going."

"Yeah, Santa," Happy said as he joined Slut by the bed, "but there were only a few of us elves left anyway. Sooner or later you would've been down to none. Then what would you do?"

Santa shrugged. "I wasn't thinking that far ahead. I hoped that if I could give Martha and myself more time, maybe something else would come along."

"Then why were you feeding us, too?" Slut asked.

Santa smiled grimly. "Why? Because the livestock needs to be fed, too, that's why. I needed to keep you all fat and healthy, so there would be some meat on your bones when your time came to go into the pot."

Steve gripped the meat cleaver harder. "You sick fuck, you'll pay for killing my brothers and sisters." He was about to move closer, and shove Slut and Happy out of the way so he could kill Santa and end this once and for all, when the fat man suddenly swung his arms around, now free of their bindings, and placed his meaty palms on Slut's right cheek and Happy's left one. Like he was clapping symbols, he slammed their heads together so hard that both the elves' heads seemed to implode, much like a ripe pumpkin would do if dropped from a tall height.

As the small bodies slid to the floor like two ragdolls, Santa roared in anger and jumped out of the bed. Handsome Joe was just standing there, staring at the carnage before him. He got in Santa's way and the fat man backhanded the terrified elf, sending Handsome Joe flying across the room. He bounced off the wall, landed on a small sofa, and rolled onto the floor. Steve watched it all happen like it was in slow motion, and he also saw Handsome Joe remain still after landing. Whether the elf was alive or dead was unknown.

Steve knew he was alone now, either way. There would be no help in taking down the fat man.

"Come here, you little shit," Santa growled. "I'm gonna squeeze the life outta ya. Then I'm gonna take your lifeless corpse and the others and have a fucking feast that will keep me in meat for months to come."

"Fucking cannibal," Steve hissed as he backed away from Santa.

"I'm not a cannibal," Santa scoffed. "I'm human, and elves are something else altogether. If anyone here's a cannibal, it's you. I don't recall seeing you pushing your bowls of stew away, and in fact, I remember you licking your bowl clean each time."

"I didn't know!" Steve yelled and ran at Santa, the cleaver leading the way. Steve swung the cleaver back and forth, hoping the blurring weapon would be enough to keep Santa at bay.

But Santa had more than two feet of height on the short elf, and his arms gave him a greater reach. It was child's play to avoid the cleaver, then reach in and punch Steve in the face.

The elf went flying backwards, his feet backpedaling to try and keep him upright. But he tripped over Mrs. Claus body and fell right on his back.

Santa laughed when he saw his opponent go down. He trod across the bedroom, his footfalls shaking the lamp on the nightstand. He towered over Steve, and with a laugh of triumph, raised his right foot into the air, his aim to squash Steve under his heel. "I'm gonna flatten you like the piece of reindeer shit you are."

Steve could only lie there, staring up into Santa's evil face. He looked into the fat man's eyes, and saw only his death. There would be no mercy from the fabled St. Nick this night.

As the foot began to descend, Steve could do nothing but close his eyes and brace for what he prayed would be brief pain, before death took him.

But just as he expected the foot to come down, Santa began to yell in pain.

Steve opened his eyes to see Handsome Joe lying across from him, his teeth sunk deep into Santa's ankle, right around his Achilles' heel.

Santa began to wobble as the only leg supporting his massive girth began to buckle thanks to the severing of important tendons in his ankle. Handsome Joe, seeing Santa was about to come toppling down like a mighty redwood, rolled out of the way, spitting blood the entire time. The elf had come to just in time to save Steve, and his quick thinking had just saved Steve from a very messy death.

Santa couldn't fight gravity, and he dropped to the floor, landing so hard that the nightstand jumped two inches before falling back to the floor. Steve knew he'd been given a precious chance to win this battle, but he had to act fast, before Santa regained his wits.

Snapping up the cleaver that had fallen from his hands, he leaped over Mrs. Claus and onto Santa's belly. "Hey, Santa, do you know what day this is?"

Santa blinked, the question taking him off guard considering everything that was happening. "No, I uh, no I don't."

"It's ten minutes after midnight. So it's Christmas day." He raised the cleaver high and began bringing it down. "Merry fucking Christmas." The cleaver sank right between Santa's eyes, going in so deep that it stuck there. Steve couldn't get it out. Santa roared in anger and pain, and Steve was thrown off Santas' belly like the fat man was a bucking bronco.

Steve was thrown to the floor; he slid across it to hit the wall, his head taking the brunt of the impact. Dazed, the elf looked groggily up to see Santa rising on his knees, before coming to a standing position. He didn't use the leg Handsome Joe had bitten, but put all his weight on the good leg.

Steve couldn't believe what he was seeing. Santa was unstoppable; there truly was no beating this mythical behemoth.

Opening and closing his hands, Santa mimicked how he was going to crush Steve within them. "Now you die, little elf."

Steve could only look up at the towering giant before him. All he'd managed to do was buy himself a few more minutes of life.

Santa managed to take one step, then his bad ankle gave out and he plummeted to the floor like the same tree he'd mimicked only moments before. He tried to put his hands out to break his fall, but he wasn't thinking about the cleaver still embedded in his forehead. When he hit the floor belly first, he teetered forward like a weeble, and his head struck the floor hard. When this happened, the cleaver was forced even deeper into his head, this time severing something that mattered, and putting out the lights in Santa's eyes in the blink of an eye. By the time Santa was done weebling and wobbling, he was already dead.

Handsome Joe was the first to his feet, and he helped Steve to stand as well.

"Thanks, Joe, I owe you my life."

Handsome Joe just shrugged. His lips were still bright red with Santa's blood. "I'm just glad he's dead." He looked over at the corpses of Slut and Happy. "To bad they didn't make it."

Steve glanced at the two fallen elves. "Yeah, it sucks, as Happy would say."

Handsome Joe gestured to the corpses of Santa and his wife. "What should we do with them?"

Steve gave it some thought, but only briefly. "I think I have an idea. Will you give me a hand?"

"Of course."

The two elves got to work.

* * *

It was late evening when Handsome Joe joined Steve in the dining room. Steve had been left alone for the entire day, and Joe had been anxiously waiting to see what Steve was doing. His eyes went wide when he entered the dining room though. He said nothing, however, figuring Steve would explain the tableaux before him soon enough.

Steve was standing at the head of the table, where Santa had once sat. In his hand was a large carving knife, and all the seats had dishes and glasses before them. "For the others. They can be here in spirit at least," Steve said with a smile, then gestured for Handsome Joe to take a chair to the right of him. "Sit here, Joe."

Handsome Joe blinked. That was the second time Steve had called him 'Joe.' He said as much, too.

"I figure Joe is good enough seems it's just you and me now. No more nicknames, no more bullshit."

"I'd like that," Joe said with a wan smile.

"You hungry?" Steve asked.

"Starving actually," Joe replied.

"Then let's eat."

Before Steve and Joe, lying in the center of the table, was a naked and cooked Santa Claus. He'd been roasted like a pig over a fire for hours, and now his skin was burnt and flaking. There was an apple in his mouth as well, something Steve had found in the back of one of the cupboards, a lucky find if there ever was one. The cleaver was still in Santa's forehead. It had been jammed in there too hard to even try and take out, the skull seeming to clamp around it like a vise. Steve didn't mind. He leaned over the table after climbing onto the chair to get a good reach, and began sawing at Santa's belly.

"I'll take some from the upper leg, if you don't mind," Joe said.

"Huh? Oh sure, of course." Steve shifted position and began cutting some 'dark meat.'

"Steve, you are aware that by eating him we really will be cannibals," Joe said in a flat tone.

Steve shrugged as he slid the juicy meat onto Joe's plate. "Not according to Santa we aren't. He's human and we're elves. Different species."

"Oh, okay then, I'm too hungry to argue that much anyway."

In the corner of the dining room, the Christmas tree was lit up, the lights flickering red, yellow and blue, while outside, a gentle snow was falling.

Steve relished the first bite he had of Santa. It tasted of justice, and of revenge—both were the same in most ways.

The refrigerator was packed with pieces of Mrs. Claus and the other elves, and Santa alone was large enough to keep the two elves fed for months. And when the meat finally ran out, the two could set off for the mainland, to see how bad the zombie apocalypse truly was.

It might not have been a very Merry Christmas for the two elves, and in fact, it was something else altogether: more like a very dead Christmas.

Steve sank his teeth into the meat before him, chewing with gusto. At that moment he decided it wasn't all bad, after all, he was still alive, and with Joe by his side, he wasn't alone.

The rest would work itself out.

*   *   *

You know, I just realized that there were absolutely no zombies in this story, which is kind of odd for a story that was supposed to mix Christmas with zombies.

"That's because you suck as a writer," Steve snapped, still sore over that 'short' jab he'd gotten back at the beginning of the story. "I've read better shit on the bathroom wall."

You know, Steve, you can really be a big dick.

"Maybe, but Big Dick is dead, so I guess it's okay."

Let's end this story, okay? I think we've said everything that needs to be said here.

"I couldn't agree more." Steve hesitated before adding, "Asshole."

Sigh.

Merry Christmas, everyone.

# ABOUT THE WRITERS

**A.P. Fuchs** finished writing his first book, "A Stranger Dead," at age 19. It was published in 2003. Since then he has written and completed many, many more books, ranging from fiction to non-fiction, to poetry and comics.

His most recent books are: Axiom-man: Outlaw; Axiom-man: Episode No. 2: Underground Crusade; Getting Down and Digital: How to Self-publish Your Book; Look, Up on the Screen! The Big Book of Superhero Movie Reviews; and Canadian Scribbler: Collected Letters of an Underground Writer.

For more on A.P. Fuchs, please visit his blog/site at http://www.canisterx.com, and sign up for his free weekly newsletter, which includes publishing and marketing tips, at http://www.tinyletter.com/apfuchs.

He can also be followed on Twitter at http://www.twitter.com/ap_fuchs

**Mariah Deitrick** is a wife, mother of four, and writer. She's a graduate from the Institute of Children's Literature, and is the author of the adult novel, "Deadly Hunt," and the Young adult novel, "The Forgotten." Her work has appeared in a variety of markets including, Spaceports, Undead Press, and Spidersilk, Knowownder!, Super Teacher Worksheets, Stories That Lift, StoryTeller Tymes, and Living Dead Press. A complete list of her work can be found at her website www.mariahdeitrick.weebly.com

**Tony Garcia** lives in the AZ mountains...safe from the apocalypse and the onslaught of zombies. "Green Christmas" & "The Zombie Who Ate Christmas" mark his fourth poke at horrific Xmas tales and sixth published story to date. His most recent works include the spirit of a serial killing clown and a blundering round-trip misadventure to Mars. Currently he is working on his first Pulp style novella about a horribly cursed pirate turned reaper! Tony draws his influences from the shadows of Howard, Moorcock, and Lovecraft. One of his biggest fans is his father, another Tony Garcia, and he'd like to dedicate these stories to him. After all, if it weren't for him...well, Tony wouldn't be here. Thanks Dad.

**Anthony Giangregorio** is the author of 48 novels and children's books, almost all of them about zombies, and has edited over 40 anthologies and books.

His work has appeared in Dead Science & Metahumans vs. the Undead by Coscomentertainment, Dead Worlds: Undead Stories Volumes 1-7, and Wolves of War by Library of the Living Dead Press. He also has stories in End of Days: An Apocalyptic Anthology Vol. 1-5, the Book of the Dead series Vol. 1-6 by LDP, Zombie Zoology by Severed Press, and two anthologies with Pill Hill Press.

He's also the creator of the 10 book action/zombie series titled "Deadwater" and the new apocalyptic series "Warriors of the Apocalypse."

**Michael D. Griffiths** is a man who likes to keep busy. He loves camping in the wilds of Arizona , playing poker, and debating such topics as mysticism, creativity, anarchy, and punk rock. He has worked with Abandoned Towers since its inception, moving from Slush Reader to Market Manager. In the past, his writing has been published in numerous periodicals and anthologies. He was awarded first place in Withersin's 666 writer's contest. He's on the staff of The Daily Discord, Cyberwizard Productions, SFReader, and writes reviews for Innsmouth Free Press. His Skinjumper Series has been chronicled in M-Brane magazine. Living Dead Press has published his novels: "The Chronicles of Jack Primus" & "Eternal Aftermath."

**Kelly M. Hudson** is the author of several short stories and two novels, The Turning and Men of Perdition.  You can find more about his work at www.kellymhudson.com

**Iktomi** lives for the splatter.  He is here to do the Devil's work.  Find him on Facebook.

**Daniel Loubier** is the author of multiple horror novels and short stories. His first novel, DEAD SUMMIT, was featured on Dread Central, BrutalAsHell.com, and was deemed, "Unusual, intelligent and highly recommended" by Jonathan Maberry (New York Times best-selling author of PATIENT ZERO and DEAD OF NIGHT). His non-fiction work includes the Eileen Dietz bio, EXORCISING MY DEMONS: AN ACTRESS' JOURNEY TO THE EXORCIST AND BEYOND. His latest novel, THOSE AMONG US, features a small family haunted by a paranormal entity. It is based on true events. An accomplished singer, songwriter and guitarist, Daniel is also the founder of the hard rock trio, Stealing Providence. Visit his website at www.danloubier.com, www.facebook.com/DanielLoubier, and www.twitter.com/deadsummit.

**Jay Mooers** completed his Bachelors of Fine Arts at Massachusetts College of Art and Design in illustration, after which he took to directing and writing stage plays, including a series of epic fantasies and a collaborative musical. He also created the webcomic Next to Nowhere. He continued to illustrate, paint murals and portraits throughout the years. In 2011, Jay completed his first solo novel, "Illweed," the success of which prompted him to begin his comic series, "Autumn Grey." With two titles under his belt, Jay co-founded Eden Park Tales in 2013 to publish these stories and more.

**Michele Roger** is an author from Detroit, taking real life places in the city and turning them into fictional horror. She is the author of the horror novel, "The Conservatory." Her latest release is "Eternal Kingdom: A Vampire Story."

**John Skerchock** professional work came first in the form of an article for Fantaco then with a horror story for Twilight Zone's sister magazine Night Cry. Work then followed with Druktenis Publishing, Horror Biz, Chiller Theatre and several websites. John also produced the classic Zacherley Scrapbook.

www.ingramcontent.com/pod-product-compliance
Lightning Source LLC
Chambersburg PA
CBHW070503120726
47910CB00003B/1106